YELLOW AMBER

AND

MISSING PERSON

BY
LINDA MCKOWN

Publisher LindaMcKownAuthor LLC

Scottsdale, AZ

Yellow Amber and Missing Person

ISBN-13: 978-1-7344095-7-4

Library of Congress Control Number: 2021913766

Author:

LindaMcKownAuthor LLC

11574 E Running Deer Trail

Scottsdale, AZ 85262

https://www.lindamckown.com

Any names of people and entities are fictitious in this story having been created by the author's imagination.

The Front Cover Photo of the book was purchased from Shutterstock. Book cover choice and editing were done by Joseph McKown.

Dedicated to young people who sometimes lose their way.

There are also the recreation vehicle owners whose crazy, last year's GPS update erroneously takes them down the wrong road. Joe would laugh at the GPS comment having been there.

TABLE OF CONTENTS

WRITER'S RESEARCH

1 YELLOW AMBER BEAD

Renee Kendra closed her notebook computer and sighed. Her new book was going nowhere. She needed a dead body, dried blood, or something. It was time to stop writing.

Her husband, Doug, noticed. He plugged in the electric pot. "The fast trip yesterday to meet the fancy lawyer at the Minneapolis Mall was unsuccessful?"

Renee looked at her husband who was preparing food for the large electric pot. He seemed to like making stew while they were at the cabin situated close to Pepin, Wisconsin. The one-inch chunks of beef sizzled. He turned them over again and began cutting the onions into large pieces.

"Don't forget, only two cloves of garlic and leave it whole so we can scoop them out."

"Got it." Doug next washed the carrots and potatoes. He began peeling.

They heard the rain start again outside.

"I like the rain. The drops sound big when they hit the roof."

Renee was tired of the sound. She glanced outside and saw bleakness. The porch was wet, and some newly fallen and slightly rotted branches dotted the very green lawn. Picking up branches was a bi-

7

weekly chore before the lawn mowing person arrived. A few branches were always missed and later were shredded by the powerful blades.

Renee looked at the rivulets running on the glass. A blue car drove by with the wipers turned on high. The white mail van stopped on the road next to the mailboxes. Five boxes stood at the new correct height and one mailbox was two feet lower. The person didn't appreciate the change requested by the post office due to the new van.

"The person is a definite non-resident holdout! Maybe they don't get much mail."

A shoot of lightning struck over the front cornfield. The sky lit briefly. Noisy thunder rolled. The rain was a normal occurrence.

"Why does it rain so much here?"

Doug started to speak and stopped. He cut the vegetables.

"Well?" asked Renee. Doug dropped the vegetables in chilly water.

"We are closer to the North Pole, and the fish like fresh rainwater. The lake fills higher, and the gigantic fish can get closer to shore to eat the tiny minnows."

The gravel road would be squishy. She missed his joke about the fish and minnows. Her mind was not registering fish now. Renee twisted a strand of hair. It was a nervous writer's habit.

"The weather seems to have caught my mood which is dark and gloomy. Getting back to the lawyer, this man has worked on this missing person case for the last twenty years. The data in his files were nicely cataloged and in date order. He was very thorough in his interviews. Mr. Rivers even has copies of the few police reports. I am amazed by his dedication. His website is fascinating to read about Amber Wood. We didn't talk long. He seemed to be in a rush regarding some case. He was a workaholic who glanced at his watch frequently."

Her husband checked his pot and was satisfied. He set the stove timer and sat down on their black leather sofa. Their apricot miniature poodle jumped up alongside him now that he was out of the kitchen with no food. The dog flopped in his comfortable spot which was the center top of the sofa. A favorite squeaky toy rested next to his nose.

"This dog is spoiled. Do you think this lawyer guy loved her? They only knew each other for approximately three months which was a bit after football season per your prior comments on the case."

She sat down on the other end. The soft pillow, rearranged to a more comfortable spot, helped her back. Renee swung her legs upon the leather footstool. She thought about her husband's question.

"Yes, I believe he did care for Amber Wood immensely. He was upset her body hadn't been found. She was only seventeen, five feet two inches tall, ninety-eight pounds, light brown hair, brown eyes, beautiful, and immensely intelligent. Amber finished high school a year early. The teachers let her take the final exams because her parents were moving back to

Minneapolis, Minnesota, to live in their old home. Amber already was enrolled in a college there."

Her husband petted the dog and wrestled with the toy. Half an ear was missing from the purple hippopotamus.

"Mr. Alec Rivers believes she is dead just like you do?"

Her fingers untwined from the hair. Renee hesitated while recalling the conversation.

"We talked about the possibility that she might be alive. There's been no contact with her devoted mother nor any of her close friends. After all this time, her being alive is doubtful. He thought she might have been coerced into meeting someone. I believe someone she knew took advantage of the situation and hurt her. The person found out she was moving and couldn't let Amber leave. We both think her disappearance and possible demise were hastily planned."

Renee looked out the window again. There was a break finally in the rain.

"Four days of rain and the yard is soaked again. Nothing is ever going to grow in this garden. There's mold on the squash leaves. I'll need to spray them with soap. The only thing that looks good is the herbs and string beans."

Seeing the sun come out, she wanted to feel better. The sunshine would help.

"I'm going to take the dog for a walk down Deer Island Road to clear my head."

She looked at him. "The herbs can be added when I get back. The tomato and steak sauce already adds much flavor to the meat."

He wasn't worried about the herbs.

"I'd rather you not take a walk. Please use the new truck to get down to the lake."

Lake Pepin was close to the cabin and less than a mile away. She was hoping for some exercise. The water was high, and it might be impossible to walk the beach. Her husband continued talking.

"That way, you will look like the normal townspeople. Everybody has a truck around here. I recommend not walking too far on the beach. Our dog isn't that brave if you run into trouble. This country does have snakes. Oh, the neighbor mentioned seeing two bobcats on the road."

Renee knew about the snakes which were further North. She did see a large tree near the road with some bark missing. There were lots of large trees where they lived and places where the large cats could live.

"Do bobcats scratch trees?" asked Renee.

"Yes, they mark their territory."

"Imagine bobcats in Wisconsin. I wonder if they look the same as the ones in Arizona. Don't answer. I'm sure they are similar only their coats are wetter."

He looked at her drily.

"See you later. I'll get the mail on my way back."

Renee looked at the dog snuggled down on the couch. Her feet slid into the rubber shoes.

Her husband mentioned, "If you are over an hour, I'll start to worry."

She grabbed her purse, jacket, and truck keys. As soon as she picked up the dog's leash, he was twirling around the wood floor barking and dancing in excitement.

"Come on dog, let's walk the beach a little way and no rolling in dead fish or else no roast beef bites."

The dog jumped into the truck the minute she opened the door.

She reached the small parking lot next to the cement boat ramp. There were cars around the small trailers to the left side of the ramp. In the summer there would be more people in the area. It was early May, much too soon for the cabins to be filled on West Lake Drive with residents or guests.

Attaching the leash to the dog, she skirted a large gray dead tree. Ants were crawling all over the log, and parts of the log broke in places. She wondered why the county didn't saw the rotten log and haul the pieces away. She walked over to one of the trailers with a small light on inside. She knocked on the metal door.

Renee introduced herself to Adele Strong. They talked about the log.

"I've called the county three times about that dead thing. They've done nothing. We think the log stinks, too."

Renee looked at the woman and said, "Do you have the phone number? I'd like to try a different tact with the officials."

"Sure, be my guest."

12

Adele gave her the phone number. Renee dialed and spoke to the man who answered.

"Hello, this is Renee Kendra, and I've noticed this dead log near the Deer Island Road boat ramp. Some kids were playing and hurt themselves. They were bleeding and crying. Maybe the county should get rid of the attraction before someone gets hurt and sues the town."

Renee nodded her head several times.

"Thank you so much. I know you people are going to do an excellent job."

Renee disconnected the call. She turned to Mrs. Strong.

"The man said a crew would be out Tuesday to take care of the dead thing."

Adele smiled. "Renee, anytime you are down here, just knock on my door if you need anything. I'll make us some tea. We like your kind of people."

"Thank you, I will. Now, I must give this impatient little dog a walk. Bye."

Renee walked close to the shoreline as the lake water softly lapped the sand. It was easy to walk the short distance to the strip of land which jutted out to a point. There was a stream of water from the old, dredged canal that stopped her. The canal had filled in over the last twenty years which seemed a shame. The water looked shallow now. She was at the end of the beach.

She looked at the almost calm lake. Occasionally, a small breeze would move ripples in the water. There were boat docks on the shore to traverse around. Later there would be more docks. She found a couple of small agates and shells. The items were placed in one of the baggies in her pocket.

On her way back a dead fish floated in the water. The dog smelled the floater and shook his head.

"The fish hasn't been dead too long. Give it a week, then you might be interested. Trust me, fried fish is way better."

The dog was yanking on the leash. The woman and her dog walked past the old tree to get to her parked truck. Her tennis shoe toe kicked something in the air. Renee stopped and stooped down. The dog wrapped the leash around her feet. She untangled the leather and held the dog tightly to her side.

"Sit a minute."

The dog sat in the cool sand. Taking another plastic baggie out of her pocket, she carefully put the round sphere in the bag. She could see the object was at one time, a small charm.

"Yellow amber is the tiny ball, I think. No, I'm positive this is amber. Good color."

Her dog approached and sniffed.

"Sit still, dog."

The dog angled closer.

"The metal must be silver. Although the metal is now black, I know I'm correct. Someone must have lost their charm a long time ago. There aren't any shops here that sell amber, especially this color yellow."

She saw some yellow-amber pieces at the Minneapolis airport once a long time ago. Now they mostly carried amethyst and turquoise.

14

Renee put the dog in the back of the truck. She went down to the beach with her phone and put the baggie with the amber bead onto the sand ground where she found the object. She took several pictures of the baggie and the distance to the trees, shoreline, and boat ramp. She walked with her feet to measure the paces and sent herself a text note.

Sitting in her truck, she remembered reading the interview Alec wrote. The interview was with Amber's mother.

Amber wore a charm bracelet with a round piece of yellow amber and other silver trinkets. The amber was expensive and cost about fifty dollars for the charm. She also wore a butterfly yellow-amber necklace. The necklace was not expensive but handmade. A friend gave our daughter the necklace. The objects must be with her.

Renee looked at the dead tree and wondered. Her imagination was running wild and way off the normal path. As a writer, she could think of a hundred reasons why something was dead. The trees were easy. They grew old. She could only think of ten reasons to explain the tiny charm.

"What if Amber Wood came here and walked the beach. She might be buried under the tree. No, a body would have washed out by now, especially during a high flood. If a body was weighted, the water would have a harder time."

Renee started the truck. She figured she was losing it big time. Still, there was the amber charm.

"Why would anyone bury Amber Wood in the sand? They would need a grader or tractor with a bucket. Someone would see such a large piece of equipment. When did Adele say the tree had fallen? She said the next spring after Amber's disappearance. Amber disappeared on April 30, 2001. There weren't too many people here that early, but the snow would have been diminished or gone."

She sat in the truck looking at the beach. Where the dead tree lay was county property. She wondered if the county would dig up the rest of the area for her.

"Nope. They would say the cost was prohibitive, and they would write me off as an escapee from the big city. Escapees were lunatics or rich. Rich was better. Money paid taxes. But taxes put in the boat ramp. I should be thankful for the ramp."

She looked at the time on the dashboard.

"I'm a lunatic for talking to my dog. You can't understand a word I'm saying. It's been an hour; we better head to the cabin."

The dog sat in the backseat. He could wait all day sitting in a truck. Her mind was stuck in repeat mode.

"Would someone be crazy enough to bury a human on the beach? Let's question the level of crazy. Crazy mild, crazy half-way, or crazy-mad. Then there's super-crazy, like a nut-job. Renee, where are we going with crazy today? Simple, I'm the sane one and an out-of-towner. Well, that explains things."

Her dog whined. She looked at the dog.

"You're the fuzzy alien from Arizona."

16

She saw her gas gauge. There was plenty of fuel.

"Maybe I can talk my husband into putting a blade on our truck, and we could dig up the beach. Wrong. Our truck's tires might get stuck."

She looked at the wet sand. Wet sand was heavier. Renee shook her head. The dig of the beach would have to be sneakier. She thought about using her grandkids and shovels.

Sorry, officer, did we dig too far down? We were building a nice outdoor fireplace, so we didn't light the trees on fire. We only wanted to burn a few hotdogs and marshmallows.

The dog's ears perked up at the word hotdog. Renee continued talking to the dog with animated hand gestures.

The officer responds to her. Holy cow, the hole almost hit China. What were you looking for?

She responds,

Bodies, maybe under the log. His eyes bulge. We don't usually have bodies buried in the sand in this county.

Renee eyed the spot near the log.

She tells the officer her theory about crazy. Her grandkids nod their heads slowly in agreement. One body is possible. He's thinking someone brainwashed the kids. Their response was unacceptable. The officer doesn't believe them.

Renee glanced at the dog who placed his head on her shoulders in sympathy.

You're arrested, young lady. Now move it.

She sighed and whispered. The dog licked her nose. She rubbed the spot and giggled, "Don't tell anyone anything, ever."

The dog barked in total agreement.

2 RETURN TO CABIN

Her husband sent her a text. She picked up her cell phone and typed a note, *Coming, the truck has started.*

Involving the grandkids in something illegal wouldn't be appreciated. She would be known as grandma-loco!

"Would that be so bad? Most grandmothers don't write about murder and disappearances. They should consider themselves lucky that I do. Imagination runs in their blood and mine."

Renee drove the way she came and parked in the large garage. She hit the garage door closer. When the door was down, she let the dog out. Waiting for the dog to finish his business in the yard, she walked into the cabin. She was calmer. Her frustrated thoughts were gone. First, she showed Doug the agates and shells.

He looked at her suspiciously.

Renee held out the second plastic bag. He saw the yellow amber charm.

Doug Kendra frowned. He hadn't expected her to find yellow amber on a lake beach.

"Your book idea just became more interesting."

"I'm afraid so."

He looked at her smiling expression.

"Oh, oh, now what?"

She circled his body. "Have you ever thought about putting a plow on the front of the truck?"

Her husband laughed. "You want to landscape the yard. It will be cheaper to hire someone for the yard.

Also, we can't dig up the county's sand or anyone else's sand. You told me some of the cabins owned the land to the water."

Renee grinned. "What about wet sand? The tires won't get stuck. The property is the county's next to the ramp."

Her husband saw right through her plan.

"No, we aren't plowing the beach, Mrs. Kendra, even if the tires are new. They would think someone was crazy. The husband is always the first suspect."

Renee smiled wickedly. He was right. Males usually were to blame. She squeezed his arm.

"I am glad you have returned safely. It's too quiet when you are gone, and the house is warmer when you are home."

"Thank you, sweetie." She leaned against the counter bar and looked at the large metal pumpkin she found to put above the kitchen cupboards. Her laundry room contained more things like a wicked black cat picture and a straw broom. Renee liked the autumnal and beach scene. Her husband didn't mind the decorations.

"Anything else happening on the lake?"

He liked to be right. He knew there was more to her adventure. This was her cue.

"You are correct. We don't want to be known as those crazy Arizona out-of-towners or that my husband is crazy good in not wanting to be a suspect."

Glad that the crazy focus moved off from her image, she went back to his question. Talking was better than thinking about the yellow amber.

"A dead fish and a few docks were in the water. I did talk with one of the campers near the boat ramp. She saw our RV in the front yard and liked the brand. We have some tiny agates and shells off the shoreline which you saw. They sparkled for a moment when the water splashed, and there's an old log which the county will remove."

Doug was surprised by all the information.

"Our RV looks wonderful in the yard, and we didn't get lost driving here. Just a little corrected recovery was necessary. The fishing season should be starting soon. Wait a minute, you picked up rocks. Great, just what we need, more rocks. Didn't we get rid of a whole bucket of rocks?"

"These are tiny ones."

She emptied the cache into an empty jelly jar, screwed a lid on top, and placed it on a shelf in the blue guest bedroom next to some of her published paperbacks. Renee returned to resume the conversation.

"Eighty miles off course wasn't too bad. We can blame the road in downtown Kansas City. The road is too gnarly for big trucks to maneuver during rush hour. I wish we would have kept some of the larger agates. They are fun objects of art or at least make good paperweights."

Her husband was already clicking the television channels. A reminder of their GPS not helping find correct directions was put to rest.

"No comment to the objects of art. I guess my husband is lost in today's worldly news."

Doug spoke, "I would buy you an amber paperweight. You like yellow the best."

Her husband was listening after all.

The yellow amber charm bag was placed in the master bedroom on top of the dresser for the moment near the beachy-looking candle holder. She played with the rope decorative ball for a moment. The yellow stone looked good in the gold and cream room. She rested her hand on the dresser's edge.

The ball represented a new mystery or a clue.

"Where are you, Amber?"

Renee was rethinking about the body.

"There's no body. No blood in the car. Why?"

She would need to purchase a silver cloth the next time she went into town to polish the silver. Renee knew there would be no fingerprints on the charm after all this time.

She regretfully stared at the piece of jewelry one last time before joining her husband. Somehow the piece was hauntingly beautiful.

"Beautiful like Amber."

The stew meat was cooked, and Renee's stomach growled. She could hear her husband release the steam from the pot. The smell was heavenly.

In the kitchen, her husband and dog were eating a piece of roast beef. She took a fork and grabbed a raw potato from the different stove pot.

"Good stew meat. I'll get some herbs from the back garden."

The vegetable pot heat was turned on by her husband. The gas flame glowed.

The dog went outside with her. She entered the large fenced garden which was an innovative idea. He liked to wander around inside and smell the leaves. The wood mulch was soft. She saw two deer walking on the edge of the property. The dog didn't notice.

"I thought poodles were guard dogs."

The dog lifted one foot and looked around. She laughed.

"Pointer dog is the latest look." The deer vanished quicker than a person's blink. Renee smelled wood smoke from the house next door. The scene was country peaceful.

"Everything is normal just like we expected. This vacation should be fun."

Cutting the herbs and a couple of the young beans, they returned to the house and food. She crunched on a bean and wondered about the past.

"More research on the book was required and digging."

She was exactly the person for the job. Personalities and murder were her specialties as an author. The evening light was disappearing. Stepping inside the cabin, she locked both doors. Renee always locked the doors. There was no reason to trust anyone.

She handed a couple of the young green beans to her husband while she chopped the herbs. He took two bites.

"These are the best green beans I've ever tasted. The wood trellis worked. I think the vines enjoy crawling on natural wood. We should return and plant some next year," commented Doug.

He took the stew meat out and covered it with foil.

"Are we making herb gravy?"

Renee reached for the cornstarch and a cup of water. He watched her swirl the mixture with the herbs. She poured the stuff into the electric pot and started the heat to a slow simmer.

"I love basil and thyme. Some fresh sage should finish the job."

She shook a few dried red peppers in the mix and tasted the beginning gravy.

"This will be perfect in fifteen minutes." She turned up the heat on the vegetables. "I'm glad you want to return. I might need to interview more people next year. Besides, the mother hasn't returned my call."

Doug tasted the gravy after ten minutes.

"Good stuff. Don't worry, Mrs. Wood will call. You have a way of bringing out the curiosity in most people."

Renee wasn't sure about Amber's mother.

3 A MOTHER'S INTERVIEW

Renee Kendra watched as the woman's housekeeper wheeled Mrs. Connie Wood into her opulent dining room in Minneapolis.

"Hello, Mrs. Kendra. I wasn't sure if you were a crank caller. Amber's old friend Alec called and assured me you would be discreet about any visit. He told me you found a charm on the beach near Deer Island Road. I was curious to see the charm and meet you. I've not heard from the local sheriff in over eighteen years. He might have died."

Renee pulled the plastic bag from her briefcase to show to Mrs. Wood.

"I believe Sheriff Edwards is still alive. His name shows in the phone book."

The old woman ignored her comment about the live sheriff. Mrs. Wood examined the small piece of jewelry. Renee needed to get her into a positive conversation. An offering of her recent actions and thoughts was necessary.

"The silver was polished by me. The charm looks better. I didn't think there would be any fingerprints. As you can see, the sand has rubbed the charm some."

The woman looked faraway and rubbed the sphere. Renee waited. She was used to waiting. Suddenly Mrs. Wood motioned to her housekeeper to bring the packet of photographs in the folder.

Mrs. Wood handed back the evidence bag. "You keep this piece of amber." The plastic was put into Renee's briefcase.

Renee opened the folder. On top was a picture of a young female in a room with yellow striped wallpaper sitting on her white ruffled eyelet bed. She was wearing a yellow amber necklace. On her wrist was the charm bracelet. A person could see the yellow amber bead.

"She just turned seventeen in that picture, and we recently moved to Pepin."

Renee looked at the young woman staring at her.

"Amber's hair has blond highlights."

"Yes, she loved the pool, and her hair would go lighter in the summertime."

Renee looked at the other pictures and stopped at the image of a male in football gear. There was a girl's handwriting on the back. She read out loud.

Rowell Blackman, best quarterback ever.

Then she moved to another picture of six girls with Amber at a slumber party. In the background, she could see a case with amber pieces.

Mrs. Wood said, "After the slumber party, one of the pieces of yellow amber went missing. My daughter was very distraught. The piece was a one-inch ball of perfect yellow amber. On the bottom was a small one-half-inch brown line. She called the line a tiny river."

Renee found another picture and looked at a close-up picture of the ball. Mrs. Wood sat thinking and remembering.

"The piece was one of her favorites. My husband examined many in the shop before he selected that particular one."

Mrs. Wood took a sip and seemed to choke on her tea.

"I'm sorry. This interview about your daughter must be hard for you."

"No, I have a cough on occasion. Old people get colds. I wanted to meet you. The fact that you author books intrigued me. Amber's collection is upstairs. We'll take the elevator."

Mrs. Wood pressed a button on a device, and her housekeeper appeared again. They entered a large bedroom with a queen-size bed. The room was lavishly decorated with expensive pictures.

The bed held a white satin coverlet and bed skirt. A gray fox fur blanket adorned the end of the bed. White wood lamps adorned the bedside tables. The white wood headboard was carved into intricate swirls.

"The fur is real."

Renee nodded. Only the best was in this room. They walked around yellow velvet chairs. The bathroom was white marble. A beautiful yellow and gray rug was on the floor. The shower was huge and new.

In the bedroom was a large glass case filled with priceless pieces of amber. Renee went to the cabinet, and Mrs. Wood sat in her wheelchair.

Mrs. Wood handed the key to her housekeeper to open the case doors.

"My husband and I traveled extensively and whenever we found some pieces, we would buy the specimen or jewelry shapes for our daughter. My husband liked to buy the individual pieces and have our jeweler in America set the stones in better quality gold or silver."

Renee saw a bracelet of yellow amber balls and a necklace with larger balls set in eighteen-carat gold. The case held mostly yellow, butterscotch, or lemon amber.

She did see a large red amber heart set in a gold wristband and heart-shaped matching earrings. There was a necklace of carved black amber roses. A bee shape with white amber stones was set in rose gold. She knew white amber was rare and noticed the bee was a pin. There were mixed strands of amber necklaces and single pendants. A plastic stand held the matching earrings.

"We bought her a yellow amber ball for her first birthday with us. She loved the yellow color. When she was six, we made the bracelet from balls we collected in our travels. There are five balls in the bracelet."

Renee counted the balls in the necklace. There were twelve yellow spheres. Amber disappeared at seventeen. Yet, there were seventeen balls in the jewelry, and then the one ball which was stolen.

"Eighteen yellow round pieces of amber. How odd?"

Mrs. Wood looked intently at her visitor. She continued her lecture regarding the amber collection.

"My husband and I decided to complete the necklace for our daughter. The shower was renovated recently along with my bathroom. I needed special hand bars and wider doors. Getting old is a terrible idea."

"Of course, I understand," replied the visitor.

Mrs. Wood turned on a fluorescent light and half of the shelf containing the amber specimens glowed blue.

Renee clapped her hands in delight.

Mrs. Wood smiled at her response.

"Amber had the same reaction."

She looked at the blue pieces more intently. On the upper shelf was the honey and more cognac-colored large specimens. She was attracted by their eerie insides. Renee was excited to see dead bees, ants, flies, plant life, and tiny bubbles.

"The more expensive specimens are the clear ones with the insects. My husband used to play a game with Amber. He would try to fool her with fake resin. She learned quickly. Then they would count to see how many insects were in each real specimen. We have one unusual piece."

Mrs. Wood pointed, and the housekeeper took out the clear piece.

"This one has the wasp and a small bee."

Renee remembered a scary dinosaur movie that used DNA from amber.

"In the movie, was it the bee DNA the crazy scientists used to make the dinosaurs?"

Mrs. Wood said, "I think they tried mosquitoes, dear."

Renee squinted and turned the specimen over.

"I see them. Their shriveled bodies are almost touching. The insects both got stuck by the gooey substance. I wonder if they talked to each other."

She mimicked the tiny insect's voice.

Hey, how do we get out of here? Beats me exclaims the bee. You're older said the bee and should know the answer. The mosquito denies that he is older and only ninety-nine million years old which is part of the Cretaceous period. The bee who is from the Jurassic period didn't fool the mosquito. Jurassic is older.

"Nope, neither one could figure things out. They were preserved forever in Burmese amber (Myanmar) sometime during the late Cretaceous period until the next even scarier movie."

Mrs. Wood continued smiling and her housekeeper nodded.

"Very good. The historical evidence is clear, and your hand gestures are original. You should have been in the theatre."

Reaching inside the case, Mrs. Wood touched a different green specimen.

"Cyrus insisted on buying this one. Amber didn't like green. I told him. Amber gave her father a big hug and said she would treasure the piece always. The color was turtle green which she liked. She was kind that way. Always wanting to keep the peace and not cause anyone trouble was her motto. There are gentle brave souls in the world, and those words would aptly describe her. Change is hard."

Renee knew she better leave soon.

"As you can see, this is the only green piece in the case other than a few charms."

There was a yellow amber box containing tiny charms of assorted colors. Renee could see a green turtle set in silver.

"He bought her a green turtle."

Mrs. Wood plucked the tiny object. Renee noticed the carefully executed etchings. The turtle looked happy. Amber's relationship with her father had been extraordinary.

Mrs. Wood turned off the fluorescent light. The housekeeper closed the glass case and locked the doors. She gave Mrs. Wood the key. They left the bedroom.

"Your husband passed away four years after your daughter's disappearance?"

Mrs. Wood looked vaguely into the air.

"His car broke down, and he decided to walk the two miles to our home. He shouldn't have walked. Cyrus never walked at all. His mind was wandering. Somewhere along the way, the police believe he encountered someone robbing one of the homes in the neighborhood. A person shot my husband and left him. His death was strange. He didn't take his pills that morning. Another strange episode for him to forget. There were no items reported missing from any of the homes. My lawyer checked. The whole story seemed wrong. Anyway, he died, and our life ended."

"I'm sorry for your loss."

Renee knew the story of Mr. Wood from the newspaper articles. She was sure the Wood household was scared by what appeared as a senseless murder. She wanted to ask about the pills, but Mrs. Wood yawned.

"Thank you, Mrs. Wood, for your time, the enjoyable viewing of Amber's collection, and the extra photocopies. You told me that you believe the yellow charm that I found on the Pepin beach might have belonged to your daughter. I'm going to hold this information from the local sheriff until I can interview more people. I hope that is acceptable to you."

Mrs. Wood appeared to return to the present with some difficulty.

"Yes, Mrs. Kendra, what would the sheriff do at this late date? Others may have purchased such a charm. If you have any further questions for your book, you can call me."

Renee accepted the business card Mrs. Wood handed her. They went down the elevator, and she was escorted out of the home. She walked the short distance to her parked truck.

Driving to a hamburger place, Renee placed her order. The waitress brought her the plate with a small salad.

She typed her notes into the notebook computer, saved her file, shut down, and placed the computer in her briefcase.

32

"During the entire interview of talking about her missing daughter, the mother didn't shed any tears. You would think there would be tears. However, the talk about the death of her husband started the waterworks briefly."

Renee tried to understand the reason. She remembered the bedroom in the over ten thousand square foot home. Her mind went back to the room. The room looked like someone could step inside and stay overnight at any time.

"Did the mother never find closure over her daughter's disappearance? The woman acted like her beautiful daughter would return. Was she in denial? Today the daughter would be thirty-seven years old. The room and yellow amber collection were in the house, waiting for Amber. Even the bathroom was updated."

Renee could visualize an older Amber wearing a white chiffon gown and her gorgeous jewels.

"Amber would be more beautiful."

She wondered how she was going to put that whole concept in the book.

"A mother waits. She never weeps until she must. She can't. What happens when they find Amber's body? Chaos is never a good thing. Delayed tears are worse. Broken hope is a killer."

Renee left the restaurant and drove home.

"One thing was certain; this woman has suffered enough."

She would need to be cautious. "No one knew what lied in the future." Renee talked to herself while driving. Talking out loud helped her logic out some of the ideas rattling in her head.

"Right now, I need a clear magic crystal ball. The bigger, the better, to see all the ghosts, creeps, weirdos, and bad people. This case was dropped by the local law due to no leads, and no experts were brought into the case. The family was rich and could afford an investigator. Mrs. Wood never mentioned hiring one. Or maybe she did and didn't want to include me regarding those facts."

She pulled over and filled the truck with gas in Red Wing, Minnesota. Next, she stopped and picked up some steaks and fruit salad at a grocery store. Putting the packages in her truck and the cold items in a plastic cooler, she left the city and crossed the bridge over the Mississippi River.

Driving the winding road to the cabin on Highway 35, she turned the music on and listened to some of the songs from her cell phone. The phone played through the truck speakers. About a half-mile from home, she pulled into a wayside rest and stepped out of the truck so she could see the view of the lake.

In the distance, she saw the white flour mill in Lake City which was across the lake about three miles or so.

The water was majestic. A few sailboats were heading toward the marinas. There were marinas on both sides of the lake. She saw some bald eagles fly overhead searching for prey.

Her day was interesting, and the amber collection was the best she'd ever seen. Yet, she felt odd and left out.

"Maybe my being in Amber's room was the problem. The bedroom vibrated with life. The bathroom was shiny new. Yet, the amber contained dead stuff and very priceless objects. I shouldn't feel excluded. Not many people have seen those rooms. Something isn't right, but where?"

She could hardly wait to tell her husband about the amber collection. Renee knew she needed to go to the Tucson Jewelry show next year and find a necklace for herself.

"Matching earrings would be nice. Some of the exhibitors would show the high-end jewelry. We don't want any fake stuff. No, sir."

There was a moment when Mrs. Wood mentioned a private thought. It was right after telling her Amber was kind.

Change is hard. "Most people would say the change was hard when referring to the past."

Renee shook her head.

"I'm being too picky about words. Anyway, it was a good interview. She mentioned a friend of Amber's named Trixie."

4 THREE CHEERLEADERS

Renee drove to Eau Claire, Wisconsin, to the address she was given. The three cheerleaders that were on Amber's team all lived within five miles of each other. The women agreed to meet the writer at Star Malone's quieter home. She didn't have any children. The other two cheerleaders were Alice Mahoney and Sheila McGrath.

Renee greeted the three women and sat down in the large family room. Coffee and small cakes were served.

"I was told the other two girls were killed in a car crash about five years ago. I'm sorry for the loss of your two friends. Did you know Trixie Moran?"

Star volunteered. "She was a cheerleader from an opposing town. We knew her from the games. Amber was closer. We saw the two talking together whenever we played their team. Amber liked most people."

Renee looked around the well-kept home.

"I'm also looking for Belinda Cummings and was wondering if you knew where she lived.

Star looked at her friends and spoke. There was a coolness to her voice.

"We honestly lost track of Belinda after high school. She wasn't our friend. We heard that she might have moved to Milwaukee and married some rich guy. No one has talked with her since senior prom night. She didn't even show the next day to get her diploma. Anyway, we assumed she graduated, but maybe not.

Belinda didn't finish her bookkeeping assignment and bragged about those facts at prom. She was terrible about doing homework and usually got her underlings to do the work."

Renee frowned. "You're saying Belinda used people?"

Alice piped up. "Yes, she was horrible. The teachers knew and did nothing. One of her minions was murdered. I think her name was Bev Dawson."

Sheila volunteered the information she read. "Her mom found Bev's body propped up on their wooden swing. The sheriff said Bev was full of beach sand. Somebody hit her over the head with a tree branch. Blunt force trauma was the cause."

Now Renee was curious. "When did Bev Dawson die?"

The two cheerleaders looked at Star who left the room and came back with an old newspaper. She flipped to page three and handed the paper to Renee who noted the date of the newspaper. Quietly she read the article and stopped.

"The coroner believed she died the evening Amber's car was left on Main Street. The local sheriff made a note in his book because he thought Amber's car should have been at her parent's home. He noted the time was nine in the evening or around there. He didn't know they were going to move. After Amber's parents returned home from their trip two weeks later, they reported their daughter missing."

"We thought Bev's death and Amber's disappearance might be connected," offered Star.

Renee nodded in agreement.

"Anything is possible. The two events look suspicious. Did you know of anyone who might have wanted to hurt Bev or Amber? Was there someone in school or any other person like a town bully?"

Sheila bit her lip. "Bev was a nobody. Her family was poor, and we knew Bev wasn't going to make it too far in this world. Aligning herself with Belinda was the wrong thing to do. Belinda was mean to people. She was always pulling dirty tricks on Amber."

"Tell me some of those tricks."

Star looked at Sheila and thought a minute.

"First, there were the ants in Amber's locker and next was the mud all over her car windows. Belinda got kicked off the cheerleading squad for making Amber fall twice during a half-time show at one of our games. Belinda blamed Amber, but Mrs. Abrams saw which one was the culprit. Oh, Mrs. Abrams was our coach."

Warning bells triggered in Renee.

"This Belinda was considered Amber's enemy?"

Alice shivered, "Yes. We all stopped talking to Belinda after she got kicked off the squad which made her even madder. I don't know why she was mad. She was at fault. We barely spoke to her before she was sacked by our coach."

Renee stood up. "I must be going. I've taken too much of your time."

Star stood. "There's one more thing. Alec Rivers was at the game, and security escorted him off the football field. I think he wanted to kill Belinda for making Amber fall. He seemed angry and out of control. Rowell Blackman didn't see the move as he was in the locker room but did hear about it later. He never liked Belinda. The falls only added to his dislike of her."

"Thank you for your honesty and comments. The newspaper article is something no one has mentioned. If you think of anything else, let me know."

Renee handed the three women her business card and left. She drove to the closest library and pulled up the newspaper article on Bev Dawson. There weren't any other articles on Bev. She printed herself a copy. She checked later articles and found the article about Amber Wood's disappearance. She printed that article.

"It's imperative that I speak with Belinda Cummings. She might be an important key."

Renee made a mental note to talk with the gym teacher and coach, Mrs. Abrams. The football player, Rowell Blackman was also on her list.

Lastly, there was a cheerleader from a competitor town named Trixie Moran. The name and address were oddly given to her by Star Malone. "My mom knows Stella."

Renee wasn't following.

"Stella is Trixie Moran's mom."

5 ROWELL BLACKMAN

The next day Rowell let Renee into his living room. Immediately she saw the gun case with deer rifles and scopes. Amber's father was shot with a deer rifle. Rowell saw her gaze.

"Hunting is what the men do around here for entertainment. My guns are the more popular brands. There must be a thousand of those types of guns in Pepin County alone."

"Are you a good shot?"

Rowell didn't want to answer, so he generalized.

"Most men in this county have been shooting a gun since age eight. What do you think?"

Renee wasn't there to talk about deer rifles.

"Who do you know that would want to hurt Bev Dawson or Amber Wood?"

"Wow, I haven't heard Bev's name for years. I wouldn't know. Bev wasn't exactly part of the in-crowd. We don't know if Amber is hurt. I hope she isn't. I hope someday she walks through my door and hugs me. I miss Amber. If that Alec guy hadn't come along, we might have married."

Renee thought Rowell was being delusional. She didn't think Amber would have married a football player from a small town. Her destiny would have been bigger. Her father would have made sure his daughter received the best of everything. However, she played along to find out more information.

"Belinda Cummings is a person of interest. I talked with Star, Sheila, and Alice yesterday. They told me about your relationship with Amber and another cheerleader named Belinda. From their conversation, there was no friendship between her and Amber. Tell me a little about this other cheerleader. If you know her address, I would be grateful. I would like to interview Belinda."

The man's brows wrinkled in a frown.

"I hated Belinda in school. Ask anyone. She was a lousy cheerleader. Out of school, we avoided each other. You could call our distaste, mutual. Belinda was a troublemaker. My senior year here was too long. She was always in my face, demanding that I tell her where Amber went. I don't know why, or where Amber went. I told her over and over until I was blue. Prom night was the last I saw of Belinda. Good riddance and I felt a huge relief."

The idea that the other cheerleader believed Amber might be alive was revealing. There were now three people in denial: the mother, the first boyfriend, and a sacked cheerleader. Two male rivals and one female adversary made for a few good chapters.

"Interesting. Belinda never contacted you again?"

He looked at Renee. "No, I left town and went to college in Madison. I doubt if she made it into college. Belinda thought she was smart. In actual reality, the girl was a C minus to D person in the grade's category."

Even with help, Belinda wasn't exactly an achiever thought Renee.

"The cheerleaders told me she had underlings, and Bev was one of her people."

"Yes, Bev, jumped whenever Belinda called."

"Do you know why Bev would have been near a beach before she died? Star let me read the newspaper she saved."

Rowell knew that Star would save newspapers regarding people from Pepin that were newsworthy.

"Yes, the sand in her clothes made perfect sense. Belinda loved the beach and would have bonfire parties. There always was a beach available. I imagine Bev was at a private party before she died."

Renee looked out the window at the trees. The lawn needed mowing. "I wonder if Bev was murdered because she saw something or knew too much?"

Rowell glanced at his lawn. The long grass didn't bother him until the mosquitos rose three feet high. He figured his neighbors were mighty pissed about the lawn.

"I'll get to the lawn tomorrow. Bev probably was assigned a task to do and failed. Belinda hated failure. Belinda might have hit her over the head in a fit of fury. I can see her propping the body in a swing as a bad joke. That's why we can't find Belinda. She's probably hiding out."

Renee was surprised by Rowell's reaction.

"Don't you think your statement is a little harsh on accusations? The other cheerleader has made you cynical?"

Rowell looked at Renee closer. The writer didn't miss much. He was wiser.

"You didn't know Belinda. She was one scary bitch and super crazy."

Renee needed to get him off his current line of thinking. He used her high crazy word to describe someone.

"You started dating Amber a month after she arrived at school when she was in the eleventh grade.

Rowell took his time. Talk about Amber was affecting him. "Dating Amber was the most fun that I've ever known. She was sweet, funny, and super smart. She was generous and liked people. The teachers liked her, too. Heck, the townspeople liked her."

Renee wrote more notes on her paper pad. She looked up at his watching eyes. "Sorry, it's easier to jot down my notes so that the story works."

He was okay with the notepad. Paper was what he liked when confronted with a problem or a new design. Paper was easily destroyed. Rowell let her know any writing didn't bother him.

"Were you angry with her when she broke off?"

Rowell looked at the ceiling.

"Yes, I was more upset with myself than angry at her. I should have tried harder. As a football player, I think that I was full of myself and wasn't paying attention. In hindsight, I'm to blame for my loss."

Renee believed him. His eyes changed to tenderness when he talked about Amber.

"When was the last time that you talked with her?"

Rowell put his hands together on his table. "I saw her after she took her last final. I didn't know why the principal let her take the exams early. That's when she told me she was moving back to Minneapolis. I asked if she was moving there because of Alec Rivers. My question made her upset. She didn't like my jealous tone."

He stared out his window and a pained look showed. His speech grew softer and slower.

"I wish. Oh, how do I wish that there was a way to go back. The one moment that might have changed things slipped through my fingers. The whole scene repeats in my mind. The loss of Amber was and is devastating. I wasn't there for her, and my pride has toned down quite a bit."

Renee wondered about his comment. Everyone had something in their past that they regretted. Failure to see the road ahead was the problem. Or at least the non-crazy people did regret the error in judgment. She continued with a different tone.

"A magic crystal ball would be nice. Unfortunately, there isn't one. You couldn't foresee the future unless you had super powers."

Rowell realized the writer was spot on to his feelings.

"No super powers here."

There was silence between them. Finally, Renee spoke, "Amber's mother told me she finished high school a year early. Amber was already enrolled in college in Minneapolis. Her future looked bright."

Rowell smiled.

"Of course, you would talk with Mrs. Wood, and she probably lives in the same mansion of a house. I told you Amber was smart. It's good to know she was ready to move down the road and concentrate on her studies. Amber once mentioned a doctor or medical degree and job might be in her future."

Now Renee was surprised. She wondered if Alec knew this information.

Rowell wanted to share with the writer one last thought. "There is something. There was a phone call from Amber. She called me from her house that last day to tell me goodbye. The time was six o'clock in the evening. Amber told me she had one final task to do. Someone found her one-inch amber ball."

Renee looked apprehensively at Rowell. None of this was in the original disappearance newspaper article.

"Someone lured her to a meeting?"

Rowell positively shook his head.

"I should have gone with her. She might be here today. I'll never know. My dad wanted some help, so I couldn't volunteer to be her escort. Again, very stupid of me."

At least she knew Rowell was with his father when Amber disappeared. He wasn't a suspect.

The living room clock gong went off. Renee jumped from the sound. Rowell didn't notice. The clock sound was familiar to him.

"After my military stint, I tried to find Amber."

Renee was suddenly interested. The clock was forgotten. "What did you find?"

He raised his hands. "There was nothing except more loss and pain."

Her disappointment showed. She put her pen down. "Before I leave, did you know Trixie Moran?"

Rowell's eyes lit. "Now, there's a name that I remember. She was an awesome cheerleader from the Raging Tigers. The team was from an opposing town. Trixie had *the moves* if you know what I mean? Lots of talent in her which made men's heartbeats stop. We all imagined a date with her in a tight dress and heels."

Renee did know. She looked at the time, said goodbye, and left. Her card was placed on his table. Rowell was again staring out the window with a blank look on his face when she closed the door.

The rain started once more. An umbrella was grabbed from her bag and used to reach her car.

"Rowell won't be able to mow tomorrow if this wet keeps happening."

She knew the lake water level would rise. This year the news stations gave the flood level readings in the evenings. People were warned to stay out of the dangerous marshes filled with trees. They were to steer slowly if boating through the main waterways because of the debris. Some of the cities were using sandbags to retain ground in the parks near the water.

The locals were found in groups in the small river towns discussing their fears regarding the water levels. Road crews were out filling in washed-out roadways. Even the trains stopped running on occasion until repairs could be done. The whistle sound was diminished at night for at least a day or two.

The large log at Deer Island was taken away to the local dump. There was a space and a hole. The hole sunk and water slowly filled and swirled around the gap. The sand on the beach shifted from the high water.

An arm bone appeared. The finger bones were missing. A man walking his large dog saw the object. The dog was restrained from getting too close. He knew the bone was human. The existing local sheriff was called.

Arriving on the scene, Sheriff Bill Edwards didn't look happy. The beach by the boat ramp on Deer Island Road was cordoned off. A small digger was brought to the area.

He scratched his head. The scene was unbelievable. Never had such a thing occurred that he could recall. The beach usually contained arrowheads and dead fishbones. There was no logical explanation.

"How did this strange body part get here? The coroner is going to have a difficult job resolving this one. Who knows how many forensics and law people are going to arrive?"

The sheriff watched as the truck and long trailer backed up into what was the parking space for the boaters.

THE PAST

6 TRIXIE MORAN

Amber waited at the small café in Durand for the out-of-town cheerleader. Over the past several months, they had become good friends even though their teams were high school rivals. Amber was glad to have found a new friend. She saw Trixie and waved her to the small booth. The girls hugged.

A waitress took their salad and soda orders. She waited and asked them about the apple pie special.

Trixie pointed at Amber to hand out their reasoning regarding pie.

"We're cheerleaders. Pie has too many carbs and is loaded with sugar. Both will slow our jumps."

The waitress looked at the two skinny teenagers and decided to argue a point that apples were good for a person no matter the size. Trixie came to the rescue.

"Look, we don't want pie today. However, that man sweating in the red shirt could probably use a slice of pie."

The waitress turned to see the man, slapped down their receipt, and hurried off. Amber put her hand over her mouth so the waitress couldn't see her attempt at suppressing a giggle.

"Aren't we glad the waitress has moved to the next customer? You are too kind. I don't mind using diversion tactics to get rid of the unwanted. Let's get back to my concerns. How did you meet this guy, Alec Rivers? He's not from this area. Did you know him when you lived in Minneapolis?"

Amber thought about her reply to Trixie. There was worry on her friend's beautiful face.

"He went to one of our offsite games. I didn't know him in Minneapolis. Someone wanted to meet him at the game. Alec has a website, and this person thought he was very cool. The person who sent him the letter signed my name. That's how we accidentally met."

Trixie stirred her soda drink. "Don't you think that was a little odd? Someone from your school signed your name on a piece of paper. He doesn't know your name but decided to show up. Wouldn't you think he would be more cautious? In the end, the joke was on both of you. What do you mean accidentally?"

Amber unwrapped her straw a little. She blew the straw paper at Trixie who caught the crumpled vertical.

"See, I know diversion tactics. Yes, I did think our meeting was odd. We would have bypassed each other. The accident was outside. I only met him because my battery was dead, and we introduced ourselves. He gave me a booster jump and followed me home to Pepin. Then he explained this strange letter."

Trixie sighed.

"Was your battery ever dead before at any other games?"

The waitress brought the salad and a basket of crackers and bread rolls with butter.

"Well, no. What are you saying exactly? Is that what you wanted to warn me about? You think Alec had something to do with my dead car battery?"

Trixie squirmed, and she fingered the basket rim.

"Let me tell you a story. I grew up in Pepin and moved away when I was eleven. My dad got a job transfer. I knew Rowell, Belinda, and the rest of the kids in the area. Belinda's parents earned money from real estate, and things didn't go too well. They sold their house and moved into a smaller one in town. Belinda dated this one guy from high school, and he dropped her like hotcakes. She tried to commit suicide."

Amber was thoughtful.

"So that's why she is mean now? Belinda is angry at the world and might have written the letter."

Trixie took a bite of her salad and Amber did the same. Her explanation would need to help her friend.

"After the suicide attempt, Belinda was worse. We're talking nut-job. Her parents stopped all controls and let her run wild. She started a gang or club or something. This gang did whatever she asked. Even the teachers were afraid of her. Then her mom died, and her dad found a new woman. If a person could go more nuts, she did. Belinda ruined her car by driving down a hill and smashing it into a fence post. She jumped out at the last minute. Her dad bought her another car."

Amber finished her salad and smeared butter on the bread roll.

'Screw the carbs. These rolls are always good."

Trixie grabbed the crackers and stopped.

"This group or gang had a way of supporting themselves once there was a leader. This leader might have encouraged theft and other unimaginable stuff."

Amber nibbled on the roll and finally put the buttered bread aside. "Belinda was content with the gang because they offered protection besides funds, and no one could ever hurt her again."

Trixie bit into the plastic with her teeth to rip open the pouch of crackers. She ate one.

"That's a subtle way of putting things. However, I do think the latter meeting with Alec might have been a setup. I have this feeling she was targeting you. Belinda sees you as the person who has everything she ever wanted. I think Belinda might have turned your overhead lights on until your battery went dead. One of my girls saw a light coming from your car when she took a smoke break. She didn't think anything of it until later when I told her your car battery went dead."

Amber was alarmed.

"Why would she use Alec to get to me? He can't be part of her gang. Also, I shouldn't be a threat to her. You are telling me this person might be orchestrating my life. Well, it's a good thing that I'm leaving Pepin after this year. She will be gone from my life.

Trixie looked up and ate her second cracker. Her hands reached for the second packet.

"Good, I'm glad you are getting away from her. My suggestion is that you do not tell her nor Alec. You need to stay away from both. As your friend, I don't want anything to happen to you. You are a good person and don't need this junk happening."

Amber took her friend's hand. The warning was received.

"Thank you for worrying and this chat. I'm good at taking care of myself. My parents have taught me that survival is important. They also made sure that I traveled with them after I turned twelve. I know how to get through many airports if I need to hide. From now on, I will be careful."

Trixie gathered her cheerleader jacket and soft leather body bag. She hugged Amber goodbye.

"When you reach Minneapolis, will you let me know that you are safe?"

"Yes, I'll send a four-leaf clover pressed in a book of poems."

Trixie laughed.

"I'll send you a four-leaf clover keychain with my photo in an expensive boat on the river. Oh, my best bikini will be on that delicious body. Take care."

Trixie couldn't leave without telling Amber a personal item. She sat down.

"My aunt told me that I could see when the earth opened a crack and closed again. Seriously, I never listened to her silliness. Something is moving. I feel terrible things are going to land. I don't want you to get caught. Tell me that I didn't just scare you?"

Amber gathered her things. She believed her friend was insightful, but she wasn't superstitious about such things.

"I think I get there is danger in the air if you say there is. We had a good discussion today about some strange occurrences, and I feel so much better."

Trixie hugged her best friend in the world and left the diner.

Amber looked at the doorway and waved to her best friend. She sat in the café a half-hour longer trying to gather her thoughts before she went home. Trixie was somehow gifted. She was a little psychic. That was what she was trying to tell her.

Amber knew the relationship with Alec would need to end regardless of Trixie's feelings. The ideas mentioned by Trixie gave her a chill. She grabbed her cheerleader jacket which she loved. There would need to be a delay in telling Alec.

"Let the earth open and close."

Amber would concentrate on studying for her finals. There were three weeks before she and her mother could move. Amber's father was away on another trip. He would be home shortly and would stop in Minneapolis first.

When she was packing boxes in her father's den, she came across a small gun with a box of shells. Attached to the box was a note to her from her father.

"Protect your mother. Use this weapon only if you need to defend against an intruder. Sometimes people aren't nice. They wear masks."

Again, someone close was warning her. Amber put the gun in its case but first, she loaded some shells into the chambers. She knew how to shoot just like she knew how to play music and dance.

This past summer, she took sailing lessons on Lake Pepin with her father. He wanted her skills to be well-rounded. The year before that she took powerboat lessons and CPR. The year before that one was horseback riding.

Amber knew her parents lavished their affection and money on her. She was always appreciative. She wondered if Belinda owned a gun.

"No, she probably used whatever was handy."

The difference between the two girls was very wide. The only thing they had in common was the fact that they were the only child in their family.

The path for one of them turned toward the dark side. Irrational behavior took over. There was no explanation for the change in behavior other than stress. Stress or extreme sadness can warp a person. Most people recover. Some don't.

The mind flips, illogical events happen, and a careless murder creates more problems.

7 ELEVENTH GRADE

Most people do somehow manage to land in the eleventh grade. There is something so perfect about this high school level. You are no longer on the bottom tier with your peers.

You walk through the halls of your school with confidence. You have made it into the big time. Calculus and basic chemistry classes are in the past. One more year and you are out of high school forever. Freedom was very nearby. A person could almost touch the sky.

Fun was yours to hold in the palm of your hands. Nothing scared the students in this class. They looked at each other with smugness. The world was their oyster. They were going to charge and take over their lives most gleefully.

The world glowed with exuberance, and life was pristine, not to mention beautiful. You were part of an amazing group of students. A driver's license sealed the deal toward the first of many more freedoms.

The kids checked out the ugly cars their parents owned and decided to get a job. They wanted the new and used sports car, not the old SUV which was rusted. The parents argued a rusted SUV was better than a buggy and a team of horses. The kids rolled their eyes. They knew their grandparents owned a Model T or Model A Ford. They saw the blurry black and white pictures on funny bent paper.

Besides, a job was cool. They got to leave the house and eat free pizza or burgers. Bagging groceries was an easy decision.

The boys did notice the girls in school classes weren't aliens and vice versa. Friendships developed and new love ran wild without any reins. That was until the girls stopped the boys in their tracks. The girls were wiser by far. They have been told to focus and concentrate on college for their future.

Their parents bought their little girls' impenetrable locks for their lockers. A few of them received new cars with massive instructions. The car keys were to be guarded against the boys.

"In an emergency, call dad and nobody else."

The girls felt strong and invincible. All things seemed fine until the first away football game.

There started the flirting with the girls by the young stags and much hot cocoa was drunk which added enormous energy fuel to overheated hearts.

The adrenalin flowed. Sweet innocent love wafted in the air. Falsehood. The boys have figured out how to maneuver the girls. The idea of love was a ruse. Like wasn't the same thing. Like was playtime.

The coaches saw the change and corralled their over-excited and enthusiastic athletes. The boys were told to concentrate on the ultimate team goal. The goal should always be focused on the game. The Pepin coaches warned them there was an empty trophy case in the school from their class. They wanted trophies in the case or else. As a bonus, the principal came and talked with the male football team.

"Hurrah, hurrah! Winning must be the only thing that should take space in my boys' brains. Education takes a backstep until there are engraved brass trophies in the case. Girls don't exist. Focus!"

The boys almost believed their coaches and principal until they saw the cheerleaders at half-time twirl and jump. The pom-poms added to the confusion. Their new skirts revealed matching and very secure panties.

The boys remembered half the message. They told themselves that they weren't attracted. They gathered in a huddle to remind themselves to focus. They were doing alright until the super cheerleaders came out and did a swishy dance. They watched the girls swing their hips and got lost in their topsides. The players became more entranced. They never saw this dance before. This dance wasn't last year's slow version at all.

The band started pumping out a new song to every step of the cheerleader's bounce. The audience cheered loudly. The noise ramped up higher. The game field was total mayhem as the opposing team finally appeared in the entrance opening. These boys seemed bigger than last year.

The Pepin out-of-town players watched the opposing team's focus and congratulated themselves.

The opposing team was also entranced by the girlie show or else they were faking it. They realized too late when the other team bared gnashing teeth. Fear entered their young minds.

But wait, there was more. Two of their cheerleaders did the splits. The girls were the top stars and showed their fists in fight mode.

The Pepin out-of-town players held their fists high in the air to show their manhood and to agree with their school's star girls.

The home team called the Raging Tigers entered the playing field with their huge body gear and new helmets.

The Pepin coach whispered. "Have they been drinking that bodybuilding wheat germ?"

The other coach responded.

"Whatever they've been drinking, I think our boys are in trouble. We look a tad thin."

The coach knew he had lost three-fourths of his team when the balls were fumbled through two-quarters of play. The lost points mounted higher. The lighted number board flipped. The coach saw the opposing Raging Tigers' number.

"The numbers can't be correct?"

The Pepin coach blew his whistle for a necessary time-out. The football team huddled around their coach with a red face. The man was fuming.

"You are a bunch of pussies. Look at this turf. The turf is smooth, yet you are tripping. I know they have those new expensive tennis shoes with the springy foam material. We'll get some next year. The opposing team put you in the girl's area to change your clothes. We found a tiny homemade camera that we threw in the toilet. To begin with, this opposing team tried to con you. Are you going to let those slobs win? You go out there and kill the jerks. There is no way they are using our women to get into your head. Our girls are better than their girls. They can do the splits and jump. Our girls dance twinkies around those slob boys."

The team quarterback piped up.

"But coach, our girls did half-time for entertainment. Aren't we supposed to watch?"

"No, you dummy. You can only watch them in class. They wear different clothes like bulky sweaters and tights under those everyday skirts. I tell you the opposing coach's cunny knows no bounds. A camera was a shameful way to get ahead. I hadn't thought of it. Anyway, you remember my words. Go fight! Go win!"

The Pepin players went out for the last attempt at a kill. There were three minutes left of the game. They weren't going to be used by any opposing team if they could help it. However, their momentum wasn't enough.

The coach congratulated himself on using psychology. However, his advice was too late. The Pepin out-of-town team lost. He groaned.

The cheerleaders were clueless they were used.

The two coaches flushed the toilet before they left. The camera parts floated to the top.

"Serve them right. They used PVC pipe for the camera attachment. PVC doesn't dissolve."

On the bus ride home, the Pepin girls looked out of the bus window. Mrs. Abrams was proud of the half-time show.

"Girls, you were amazing. Your excellent practice showed. Now we need to come up with a plan to knock the other cheerleaders out of the park."

The cheerleaders were tired. They did a good show, but their boys lost. They wondered how the boys could lose. The girls agreed their boys were ill-prepared. The other boys were hunks of muscle. Their boys looked pale and wasted.

The cheerleaders would snub their hometown boys for two weeks.

The Pepin boys would learn their lesson. They needed to build some muscle. Eleventh grade now meant war. Fun was over for the town's football players. They would kill the next team if they didn't win. They won every game after that.

The coach loved one person on the team, and this person was the differential that existed. The boy was an over-achiever and talented. The sheriff told the coach to keep the team's eyes focused on this homeboy.

"He's super good and has a brain!"

This boy held private training sessions with the rest of the team near the public beach. They ran the length of the beach and the railroad steps ten times a day to build their muscles.

The team practiced additional plays the coach wasn't aware of. The hometown boy was the up-and-coming quarterback named Rowell Blackman. He researched and watched all the games on the television set. He wrote down new plays and drew diagrams on paper. Rowell wanted to win. Losing meant failure. He didn't want to leave his high school as a failure.

The cheerleaders noticed Rowell. He was a born leader. Eleventh grade was only the start of his career. Rowell didn't fall for complacency. He knew the world didn't automatically belong to you. A person needed to fight or not survive.

There was one cheerleader he noticed. She was a new girl. She could do the splits. His heart fell hard.

Rowell became a star in his hometown. There was only one reason to push to the ultimate. He wanted Amber to notice him. She finally did. Then she disappeared. He took the college route and the military.

Rowell later was awarded medals afterward by his country for fighting major strongholds. He went home and packed the medals away. His parents were proud. The medals weren't as important as the eleventh-grade medals he won. Those medals were in the school's large case with his jersey and picture.

He never told anyone about the country medals.

His friend, the newly elected sheriff, talked with Rowell's dad one evening.

Sheriff Bill Edwards knew who Rowell was. Rowell was his friend, a favorite hero of their small town, and a very qualified real hero of his country.

8 FIRST MOVER TRUCK

Belinda Cummings drove to Wabasha to get groceries. She was tired of eating food at the local gas station. Plus, she developed a plan for a small beach party. It was time to force someone to acknowledge that she ruled this town.

Her car drove past the large four thousand square foot house where Amber Wood lived. She glanced at the house and saw a heavy truck. She couldn't see any words on the side of the truck.

Reaching the *"Y"* in the road for the turn to Durand, she pulled into the small park and ride space. She tapped her fingers on the steering wheel of her car. Belinda wondered why there was an oversized truck sitting on the road.

Amber's house was the only house on the private dirt road.

"Maybe they are getting more furniture or a new lawn tractor. There could be any number of reasons for the big truck."

Belinda pulled out of the parking area and drove to Wabasha. She picked up a foam cooler, some long metal forks, paper plates, hotdogs, buns, potato chips, dip, ketchup, and relish. She also grabbed a box of wood stick matches. Then she drove to the pharmacy and picked up the sleeping pills for her father. She took seven pills out of the bottle and hid them in her pocket.

Leaving the grocery store, she went to the liquor store and was going to buy a six-pack of glass bottled beer. She put the beer back and then grabbed the beer. She dropped the container on the counter, threw down a ten-dollar bill. She showed her fake ID. The woman gave her the change.

"Do you carry root beer in bottles?"

She was told Durand was the closest place. Belinda sighed.

She checked her glove compartment to make sure the bottle opener was inside.

Next, she drove to the hardware store in Wabasha and bought some plastic tarp and nylon rope. There were only two boat anchors. Belinda bought those anchors, and the clerk sold her the metal clip and showed her how to splice the rope to attach the clip.

On the way back she drove over the large bridge and looked down at the Mississippi River. The water appeared to be flowing fast.

"Good spot to jump off or dump a body."

She drove to the cheese store and bought an ice cream cone in Nelson. On her way to Pepin, she suddenly turned toward Durand. Finding the root beer in the grocery store was her last task.

On the road into the Pepin, she glanced at Amber's house. The large white truck was gone.

"No big deal, the truck is gone."

Reaching home, she put the hotdogs, dip, and beers in the refrigerator. The rest of the stuff was left in a plastic bag on the counter. Her dad wouldn't bother her stuff. He was at his girlfriend's house. She put the bottle of pills on the windowsill where he could find them.

She called Bev. "How much have you gotten done on my bookkeeping assignment?" Bev told her she was halfway done with the booklet.

"Why are you only halfway done? You told me you knew this stuff."

Bev whined that the work was harder than she thought, but she was going to get some help.

Belinda was angry and pounded on the counter. She picked up the plastic glass and threw it at the door. The plastic glass cracked into several pieces.

"You will get this homework done today."

She hung up the landline phone. Slowly, she picked up the plastic pieces. Belinda ran the ragged edge against her wrist scars.

Angrily she threw the pieces in the garbage and called her contact.

"I bought the groceries and liquor. As soon as I can, I'll extend the invitation to the party."

Belinda didn't tell the person about the sleeping pills. The pills were for her protection. Suddenly, she didn't trust the new person. Belinda was doing fine until this person entered her life. It was a decision she shouldn't have made. She might need to terminate more than one person.

"The two would look logical together in death."

Belinda went upstairs and found the one-inch yellow sphere and put the ball in her blue jean jacket pocket. "A little amber to taunt Amber."

9 FINALS

Amber sat in the principal's office. She finished her exam and handed the paper to his secretary.

"Your last exam is tomorrow at ten in the morning. Your math teacher was concerned about letting go of his precious exam. The principal assured him that you would not divulge the test questions."

"No, ma'am, I would never do such a thing."

The secretary winked at Amber.

"Honey, you and I know that you can pass his silly test with your eyes closed. You can calculate in your head. There isn't one student in this school that can do that move except for Rowell. We'll see you tomorrow."

"Thanks, Ms. Roxy. I'll be here. My housekeeper said she would make a pan of cinnamon rolls early. I'll bring you and the principal one."

"Bless you, child."

Amber left the principal's office and ran into Rowell.

"Hi. I stopped at the principal's office to ask them a question about colleges."

Rowell looked at her suspiciously. She did talk to the principal about the college he attended, so technically she didn't tell a lie.

"You know someday I'd like to go into medicine. College is important."

"Sure, and I think medicine is a good field. Would you like to stop at the hamburger place for lunch? I've got some money from jobs for my dad. I'm half done."

Amber was tempted to eat lunch with Rowell, but there was no reason to go down that road.

"No, I promised my mother that I would help her move boxes around at home. We're sorting through clothes to donate. A lady friend is going to come by the house and will drop them off in Durand at the thrift store."

He looked disappointed and waved. "Okay, I'll see you in class tomorrow." Rowell left the building.

She almost ran after him to tell him that she wouldn't be in class, but she stopped herself. She remembered Trixie's warning about being careful.

The next day, Amber completed her math final and went to the gas station to fill the tank of her mother's car. She was surprised to see Bev Dawson staring at her.

"Hi, my mom needed a favor," said Amber at a not so astonished Bev.

Bev moved closer. "Don't worry, I won't tell them that you skipped school. I called in sick. I was trying to finish a bookkeeping assignment. It's funny that I ran into you. I did see your car at the school for a brief period. I figured this was a good place to watch traffic. There is a party tonight at eight o'clock on Deer Island by the boat launch. Count yourself as officially invited."

Amber frowned. Bev was looking for her. The meeting wasn't accidental. She meant to ask her to the beach party. The question was, "Why?"

Bev saw Amber's hesitation and decided to up the ante.

"Some of the kids chipped in money for beer and hot dogs. There's also root beer. All you need to bring is a bag of cheezies or donuts. Belinda told me she found something of yours. She'll bring the object. Please, please say you will come."

Amber paused before putting the gas hose back. "Did she say what she found?"

"No, she wouldn't tell me." She whispered, "The object is round and yellow."

Amber remembered her pajama party and the next day when an object was missing from her glass case in her bedroom. She responded, "I'll think about it."

"Great! Don't be late, okay?"

"Right, eight o'clock, I'll remember."

Amber drove home and parked her mother's car in the garage. This might be the only opportunity to retrieve her precious yellow-amber ball. However, she needed to develop her plan of safety.

She went into the house. Her mother was putting two sandwiches and some bottled water in the refrigerator.

"We've gotten the last box all taped shut. The mover truck should be here any minute. I saved two sleeping bags for us. The realtor will let the cleaners in. I'm to leave her a key in the metal punch box on the door. In the morning, we can get up early, find a restaurant, and head to our home in Minneapolis."

"Great, mom. We finally get to leave this town. Won't you miss your garden friends?"

Her mother nodded that she would.

"I'll miss the milkweed plants along the property line. I hope the new owners keep them. I loved helping the butterflies."

Amber hugged her mother.

"I have to go out a little later. There's a hotdog party on the beach near Deer Island. I'll try not to stay too long."

"You go have some fun before we leave. Make sure you take a warm jacket."

There were clothes in her room on the doorknob. Amber retrieved them. "I've got my black nylon hoodie and black sweat top. Did you save my black hiking boots out?"

Her mother pointed toward a backpack sitting next to the door.

Amber looked inside. The boots would be warm. She wasn't sure the party could be called fun. Amber would rather not go anywhere near Belinda.

She thought about calling Rowell. Amber didn't want to involve him. Amber called him anyway. He was busy with his father. The beach party wasn't mentioned. She would go alone and get to the area early. Buying some packages of little donuts containing cinnamon sugar, her treat was easy to purchase from the small store in town.

10 BEACH PARTY

Her car drove onto the cement ramp. There were no cars in the small parking lot. There were no vehicles around the few remaining travel trailers on the left side of the ramp. Amber left home shortly after six o'clock. She needed to remain undercover. The party idea gave her the chills.

Amber drove down the small road to the end. There were no people in any of the raised cabins or on any of the back lots. The entire west side of the island was deserted.

"This is a perfect place for a disaster to occur."

The light was dimming. She didn't turn on her car lights. Amber drove to one of the cabins. She brought her mother to this cabin for a garden club meeting. The cabin was nice inside.

The cabin owner's parking lot at the time was full of cars, so she drove into the driveway of the next cabin. Some of the cabins owned a small boat ramp.

The place looked to be the perfect spot. The boat docks were out of the water on the cement. There was a small space between the boat docks large enough for her car. She drove into the spot.

In her rearview mirror, she saw the outhouse. The outhouse hid her car as did the boat ramps. She could easily drive out of the spot. Amber waited for an hour and a half. She saw car lights drive down to the county boat ramp where the party was to be held. Amber waited another half an hour.

There were no more car lights. She waited for fifteen extra minutes. No other vehicles appeared on the road. Amber felt her bladder pushing. She stepped inside the outhouse and used the facility. Fortunately, she carried a tissue in her pocket.

Exiting the outhouse, she grabbed the plastic bag of donuts and worked her way through the cabin backyards toward a small bonfire on the beach.

Amber climbed under an aluminum boat where she could listen to the conversation. The donuts were close to her head.

Belinda was hollering at Bev. They were the only two people at the party. Amber saw the cooler, the beer, and the hot dogs. Bev was cooking her dog. She wondered why no one else was there. Amber figured out Bev lied to her.

Belinda fumed, "You told me Amber would be here. Where is she? She's late."

"I don't know where Amber is. I'm not her keeper. She said she would come. Get off my back."

"You are lying. Why are you lying?"

"I'm not."

Bev put the burnt dog in a bun and poured ketchup on the bun. She ate the entire meal, the potato chips, and reached for a root beer bottle.

Belinda uncapped the bottle for her. She uncapped her beer bottle. She dragged a large wood stick closer to the fire. Belinda started throwing potato chips into the fire and watched them sizzle. The more chips she threw, the more the minutes ticked past. She threw the bottle caps and empty bags at Bev who complained.

Amber stayed hidden. She was worried the party was somehow a trap. Belinda seemed pissed off and probably didn't bring her amber sphere.

She whispered to herself. "This is a very bad idea. I need to leave." Amber was going to crawl out from the boat when there were feet outside the boat. Someone was peeing on the ground. She stayed hidden.

The man walked away, and she heard an engine start far down the road. She figured the person was also invited to the party and changed their mind as did she.

Belinda was shouting louder at Bev. Amber felt uncomfortable. Bev started crying and waving her hands. Amber tried to see the time. She thought her dial read nine o'clock. Peeking under the boat, she quietly pushed the weeds out of the way to see better.

Amber was struggling to rise. Her boot caught in the boat seat, and she looked away. The donut bag was forgotten.

Suddenly, Belinda picked up the large stick and hit Bev in the head three times.

Amber heard thumps and almost screamed. She couldn't wait and rapidly freed her boot. There was dead silence. She kept her head down. After a few minutes, she heard glass bottles clanking and a person's feet running on the rocks near the shoreline.

Now Amber was scared. She crawled out and looked toward the car. The night was dark. Someone inside lit a cigarette. Belinda smoked. There was possibly one other person in the vehicle. It was hard to see. She hoped it was Bev. The car drove away.

Amber stumbled toward the bonfire and saw Bev on the ground bleeding from a head wound. Her root beer bottle was empty. The liquid made a small spot in the sand. She lifted Bev's arm and checked for a pulse. There was none.

Amber tried the other arm and next she tried the neck. The face was still, and the eyes were staring. Bev was dead. Amber looked around and felt for her amber butterfly necklace. Alec gave her the present. She was nervous and kept pulling on the necklace. Not realizing the necklace ties came loose, her necklace slipped to the ground. Her hand snagged on part of the stick. Amber yanked free. The tiny charm laid in the sand.

Amber jumped at a bird sound and ran.

The cabin where she parked her car seemed far away. Her breathing was shallow. She stopped by a tree of hanging dried gourds and ducked under them. Touching her car metal, Amber opened the door and quietly closed it. Starting her car, she drove down the short road and turned left at the corner. She drove fast and then let off the gas as her car flew over the railroad tracks. She cranked the wheel to the right. Her car tires squealed.

Amber was on the highway, heading toward town. She parked her car on the main street being careful not to hit the high cement curb.

"I should tell someone what I saw. No, I can't. I didn't see it happen. There might have been someone else who saw what I heard. What to do?"

Locking her car, she sat in the front seat although everything inside her told her to run as fast as she could. The enemy couldn't find her if she ran.

11 PARKED CARS

Amber couldn't stop trembling. There were a few cars on the main street beside hers. She saw the sheriff's car turn the corner. It was the perfect opportunity to reach for help. Amber ducked down. The sheriff drove slowly past and turned right at the corner to drive down to the pier on Lake Pepin.

She sat upright. The shaking had diminished some, and her breathing returned to normal. Amber realized she heard a murder and was a witness.

Automatically, she reached for her necklace. The yellow amber necklace with black cording was missing.

Amber groaned. She realized where she lost the necklace.

"The police will believe that I killed Bev. Belinda will twist things her way. She always does that move. I'll be the one put in prison. My father, I must talk with him. He will know what to do. The phones have been disconnected at the old house."

She looked in her coin purse. There were no quarters for the phone booth on the main street.

"Think, Amber, get your act together. You didn't create this mess. I should never have gone to the beach. What was I thinking? Belinda will know that I know she is the killer. Maybe not. But who was the second person in the other car? The person who peed, of course. Men stand up when they pee. Who was the man staring at the party?"

She didn't know.

"He left before dreadful things happened. The man never saw me."

The whole town knew she wore the necklace. Amber believed she was in danger and so was her family.

"I promised to protect my mother. Oh, god, I must get her away from here. She's alone at the old house."

Amber checked her car and stuffed items into her bag.

"Run, Amber."

Amber snuck into her old house and awakened her mother. Earlier she stuffed the sandwiches and water in her backpack. They folded the sleeping bags and put them in her mother's car.

Amber's mother drove to a hotel across the lake and checked in. Her mother called her father. They hung up and waited. Her father called back and told Amber the plan after doing a hypothetical with his lawyer that evening.

Amber trusted her father and followed his directions. She was always his little girl. She tried to be good. Her eyes watered.

"I messed up."

Mr. Wood sat in his expensive home in Minneapolis. He lit the fireplace and watched the wood ignite. Amber's safety was what mattered the most to him and his wife.

No one was going to hurt his daughter. Especially, not a creepy girl and her weird boyfriend.

The father was angry. This year was supposed to be enjoyable. The idiot girl ruined things. He knew her name and wouldn't forget it. This was the time to fight back silently. He was very skilled and adept in his world. Mr. Wood would play the waiting game.

Her father knew eventually bad people either were caught or were killed. Mr. Wood needed to be exceptionally alert. He would prepare Amber for all worst-case scenarios.

When the body of Bev Dawson was found, Mr. Wood knew his decision was a correct one. There was no mention of the yellow amber butterfly necklace. Someone kept Amber's necklace. The father never liked the necklace. The yellow amber was a low grade.

Mr. Wood thought about the young girl who was dead. He didn't know her or her parents.

He was grateful his daughter was alive.

12 THE PROM DANCE

A year later, Belinda dressed for prom. She found the perfect dress. The mirror reflected her image. She couldn't stop looking at herself. The dress was navy-blue pleated satin. The neckline was high with a ruffle and the back was incredibly low.

She put navy-blue flats on her feet. The shoes were a little tight.

"There's no need to look taller than the football players."

She went with some of her underling females. They didn't need a date to go to the prom. There was always the afterward part. After the prom, she was meeting someone. Belinda was excited about the noise from Amber Wood's disappearance. Bev Dawson's murder naturally died down.

She slipped the necklace under her collar and tied the black laces. Belinda adjusted the yellow amber necklace, so no one could see the gems. No one knew she found the piece of jewelry when she returned to the beach.

Mrs. Abrams, the girl's gym teacher, saw Belinda enter the gymnasium. Mrs. Abrams pursed her lips in distaste.

The teacher shook her head. She felt the wrong person disappeared last year. Amber Wood wouldn't for one minute hurt a fly, and Belinda was besmirching Amber's name every chance she could get.

Mrs. Abrams saw the football players step away from Belinda and disappear outside if she got too close. The rest of the boys remembered the tenth-grade biology class experiment and hid in the men's room. The cheerleaders ignored Belinda. For a second she felt sorry for the girl.

The DJ started his music, and a few couples took the dance floor. After two hours, Mrs. Abrams developed a headache. She wanted to go home but she was one of the school chaperones for the evening.

She went into the restroom and ran into Belinda in the lounge area putting on hot pink lipstick. Next, she watched her comb her long straight black hair. Belinda moved her head and that's when Mrs. Abrams saw the black cord and the smaller yellow amber beads.

Belinda let her hair relax and left the restroom.

"Bye, Mrs. Abrams."

Mrs. Abrams sat down in the only chair in the room. She thought she was going to have a heart attack. There was a phone in the office. The principal's office was locked. She needed to lie down. Another teacher saw how ill Mrs. Abrams was, and she drove her home.

Mrs. Abrams took off her dress and shoes and put on her soft, ratty pink bathrobe. The bathrobe was like a comfortable old friend. The pockets were worn, and the color was faded. Mrs. Abrams felt faded and sad.

"Should I call Sheriff Edwards and report what I saw?"

Mrs. Abrams knew the necklace was Amber's.

"Belinda would lie and tell everyone she bought the necklace at a flea market. I would be blamed as a nosy old busybody."

Mrs. Abrams was always a jolly person. Now, there would be no joy in teaching. She dug out her bank account.

"I should retire." She knew there wasn't enough money.

"At least Belinda will be gone. The accounting teacher told me that Belinda did turn in her bookkeeping book for her second term. I wonder who completed that assignment. It doesn't matter. She can cheat her way somewhere else."

Mrs. Abrams was glad she didn't have to attend the commencement ceremonies. Her face would give her feelings away.

She thought about Amber and how the girl could bend and do all the jumps with great ease.

"Amber was like the butterfly. Maybe the necklace is a message. I hope Amber is alive."

Mrs. Abrams went to bed feeling slightly better.

13 PROM NIGHT

Belinda went to the beach. Her clothes were changed into blue jeans, and she wore her old cheerleader jacket and a dark T-shirt. Her suitcase was packed and sat in the car trunk. The man told her to be ready. He didn't exactly tell her what to be ready for, but she guessed.

"He will naturally want me to live with him. I'm a graduated senior now. My life will change."

A car parked next to hers. The water was high again, and the small trailers were gone from the area on higher ground. There were only a few lights in some of the cabins. The lights weren't bright. They were LED night lights. Belinda didn't mind being in an area devoid of humans. She wasn't afraid of anything.

"The blanket. I need a blanket. She brought the blanket from her car with some beach towels and started the fire with her matches. A rope from her messy car stuck to one of the blankets. She heard a noise and turned. The man joined her.

"Did you bring the pills?"

Belinda was disappointed that was his first response to her. She opened a root beer for him. She knew he didn't drink.

"I'm sorry you missed the prom dance. My dress was super beautiful. The football players enjoyed the navy pleats when they danced with me. It's hard to be the only beautiful woman in the room. My teachers were amazed at their A-student."

The man didn't respond. He knew bullshit when he heard someone lying through their teeth.

Belinda handed over the bottle of sleeping pills. He sipped the cold root beer and took one pill out. He dropped the pill into her bottle of beer.

Belinda was confused.

"Hey, why did you do that? I don't take medicine. These pills are strong."

The man smiled.

"You are way too uptight. There is plenty of time to get to know each other. I received your note. You have something for me. You mentioned the object was valuable."

He leaned over and kissed her on the cheek. The man didn't want to kiss her but knew this was part of the game. This game would appear friendly on the surface.

She grinned and relaxed. She could feel the pill working. It was worth the drive to Durand to buy the man his silly root beer.

She took a sip and thought the man was strange tonight. Belinda decided to give the man his gift early to break the ice. She pulled the yellow amber ball from her pocket and held the object out to him. The ball almost glowed from the firelight.

"This is my gift to you. I found the object in a specialty shop in Stockholm. They sell old stuff. This is old. I think the lady told me rarer if the ball was a solid yellow. The brown line makes it cheaper."

The man hesitated and slowly took the sphere. The amber warmed in his hand. He could imagine a young teenager holding the object. He tenderly put the object in a zipper pocket.

"The lady was wrong. The brown is important."

Now he knew what Belinda was besides a young girl's killer. She was a liar and a thief. Was she the cause of Amber's disappearance? The man would make his decision. He needed a few more minutes. He was glad the pills were strong.

When she wasn't looking, he added a few more pills to her bottle. Then he saw the amber necklace and knew there was no return. The man hated her. His eyes smoldered with revenge. Belinda was in grave danger because she was guilty.

The man looked at the water against the shoreline. The embers in the fireplace died down.

"I'll get you some more firewood before I leave."

Belinda couldn't believe the man was leaving without her. Her mind raced.

He went to his vehicle to get a hatchet. He would drag a log and chop more firewood for her before leaving. There was a box of tools in a soft bag. He fumbled for the right one. His hands touched the sharpened object. The outer case was removed. He took the device out of his trunk.

The man returned, took a sip of his root beer, and chopped a few pieces of wood. He took another drink and threw two pieces on the fire. Belinda was smiling weirdly. He figured the pills were working on her.

Suddenly, he grabbed his stomach and fell to his knees. He realized she put something in his drink. The man fell over and passed out.

After an hour, he came to with a jerk. He saw her arm wrapped in a towel with a rope tied around. The man moved the towel, saw the deep cut, and realized the woman could bleed to death.

"Oh, man, she must have cut herself by accident. The arm looks bad."

The keys were retrieved from Belinda's pocket. He drove her car to the Wabasha emergency parking lot and placed a lump wrapped in a towel and blanket in a wheelchair. There was no identification on her. He stopped.

"What if she tells the people at the hospital that I tried to kill her. I didn't, but she is evil. The police would arrest me, and all my dreams for the future would be stolen from me. Well, guess what? Nothing is going to happen to me. I will deny everything."

He was wasting time. Pulling his hat down further, he checked to make sure he wore gloves. The wheelchair was pushed to the door. The man pressed the bell and disappeared.

He wasn't going to take the blame for this bad business. The thought occurred to him there was a possibility she cut herself on purpose.

"In which case, the woman was a nut-job."

He ducked down in the car. When he thought the coast was clear, he drove out of the parking lot. After ten minutes of driving around Wabasha, he drove over the bridge. There were no cop lights in his rearview mirror.

The man returned to the bizarre scene and hastily picked up the garbage. Next Belinda's car was sunk into a marshy pond. A few mosquitoes buzzed. There would be no problem if the car were found. He wiped his prints.

"I hate mosquitos." The man swatted at a few and jogged back to the boat landing and beach. He took one last look around. The bag was dumped into the trash can. His hatchet was cleaned in the lake. The sand was kicked over the fire. The area was in total darkness. He threw her car keys in the water as far as he could. The charm pressed deeper into the sand by his heavy foot.

"No one will care what happens to you. I certainly won't. If you ever remember this night, it will be too late. I wasn't here. My career will move me away from your downer small-town life permanently. How could I have been so stupid to see this woman? She tricked me."

He felt the round sphere in his pocket.

"At least I have the treasured ball and the necklace. She won't remember either one."

The man drove away. He was sure of himself and comfortable in his skin. No one knew he was ever on the beach. He took Amber's necklace off Belinda at the last minute. Now all he needed to do was find Amber.

"Amber must still be alive. Why doesn't she call me or appear? I was her friend. She must know."

Belinda's car sunk lower in the muck. The mud did fill every crevasse. Suddenly a large air bubble shoved the car to the surface where the hood tilted, and the vehicle flipped over. The four bald tires finally disappeared from human view.

The engine oil filled the swamp with an oily coating. The noisy mosquitoes avoided the oil and flew somewhere else

They were smarter than Belinda by far.

The man reached his destination. A sudden thought occurred to him.

"I should have let her die."

He pounded the steering wheel. His last-minute decision to save the woman would create havoc. The woman would rise with renewed resilience.

"Too late."

14 RESURRECTED RESILIENCE

The hospital doctors agreed. The young woman's arm wasn't healing properly. They scheduled her arm removal surgery.

After ten days in recovery, she appeared lucid but told them she couldn't remember her name.

Five days later, the hospital cold storage room key was stolen. A break-in occurred. After checking the list and items in storage, they found the young woman's arm appeared to have been stolen. The items in the room were scheduled for destruction through a local crematory. There was a delay in pickup.

The nurse informed her boss of the loss.

"There's no logic as to why someone would remove an amputated arm from this building," complained the nurse.

The doctor responded, "The floor nurse saw a strange teenager carrying a large gym bag. She walked in and out of the hospital on the same day of the disappearance."

"How odd? Do you think this thief knew our Jane Doe?"

The doctor rubbed his brow.

"We'll never know. The person wore a baseball hat, sunglasses, blue jeans, a tank top, white tennis shoes, and tan gloves. The teenager looked normal."

"Too bad."

He frowned. "The nurse told me there were words on the tank top, "*Get Lit*!"

Now the nurse frowned.

"*Get Lit* as in fire?" The nurse wondered about their patient who might have strange friends. Strange friends could mean trouble.

"The patient may be hiding a different personality."

The doctor started to walk away.

"Your guess is a good one. I'll be glad when we can get rid of the Jane Doe patient. She's trouble with a capital *T*. Anyway, I've got to do my report for the police, not that I think they will ever find the arm in this century."

The nurse also would be relieved.

"Oh, let's not disclose our thoughts on personality in her file."

"Yes, doctor. Jane Doe might be fine."

The female patient got worse and more reclusive. The doctor thought she might have had a stroke. Their only choice was to send the Jane Doe person to a nursing home in Rochester, Minnesota, to get well from her surgery and receive proper therapy.

When she was better, the woman still hadn't responded to any of the nursing home staff's questions about her identity even though she was asked every day.

Hence, the staff kept her name in their computer file as Jane Doe. Her file was assigned a number and cross-referenced to the hospital case.

Years went by and the woman didn't talk. It was as if the person inside the body disappeared into a cloud or a different world of her own making.

Jane Doe lived in a nursing home for twenty years. She did become ambulatory and walked around the facility with a cane. Her favorite pastime was watching the game shows on television or any show with canned laughter.

She used the cane even when she no longer needed one. A weapon was important to her. She didn't tell the staff.

On occasion, she would play cards with the staff and lose. She would shake her head yes or no and use her righthand fingers to indicate the number of cards she should receive.

The staff believed she was almost ready for release. A problem existed. They didn't have any person to release her to. There appeared to be no relatives of her family left nor friends. With her inability to speak, they were stumped.

Then one day she was watching a television newscast when she started shaking violently. The staff believed she was having a seizure. Her mouth foamed. They strapped her in bed for three weeks. Once they released her, she appeared to be fine.

The next morning, they found Jane Doe with pins all over her face and the top of her arms.

Jane spoke, "Acupuncture."

The nursing staff removed the pins and sent her to their psychiatrist. While he was talking with her, a fly landed on his desk, and Jane took out a hammer from her pocket. She started swatting the fly with the hammer.

Quickly, the security guards restrained her and took Jane back to her room. She was again tied to her bed.

At lunchtime, she was put in a wheelchair and taken to the cafeteria for her meal. Today was chocolate pudding day. Jane grabbed three dishes of chocolate pudding from the cold food area. The worker relented and let her have the pudding.

Jane sat by herself. The worker left her alone to eat. When he returned, the windows of the cafeteria were smeared in chocolate pudding. Jane sat serenely with chocolate all over her hands.

The nursing staff saw the mess, and Jane was locked in her room. There was an emergency meeting of the board. The board talked about the strange woman for over two hours.

"Jane Doe was like a dead person when she arrived. Suddenly, she awoke. We were excited and believed she was resurrected. The thing is we have a bigger problem. She's crazy at the extreme level."

One of the board members commented. "Can we put her back?"

The board looked at the doctor in the room.

"Drugs would work, but she might hide the drugs. The flowerpots in this building are full of pills."

Another board member replied, "Let's get rid of the pots and give her massive drugs."

The doctor shook his head. "We don't know how much drugs would keep her calm again. Besides, I could get into trouble. You need to get rid of her, or she might kill someone at your facility. You would be responsible."

The board voted, and Jane Doe was to be transferred to the nearest available mental hospital.

A hush overcame the nurses who attended to Jane. They refused to look her in the eyes. Jane knew something was wrong. She needed to escape as soon as possible.

Every day she watched. In the morning, she saw the nurses came into the building through the back door. She needed clothes and a weapon to escape. There were closets in the other patient's rooms. Her room didn't have a closet.

Jane slipped into a patient's room and found a pair of sweatpants and sweatshirts in a gift box. She ripped the tags off and put the plainest outfit on. The cane was thrown in the closet. She tied her hair up and grabbed a pair of sunglasses in the lost and found. There was a large plastic bag which she also took.

Jane saw Nurse Macken put her car keys in her pocket before opening the back door. She was ready. Using the large bag, she bumped into the nurse and stole her car keys.

"Excuse, excuse," said the woman in the sweat outfit. She was carrying a potted plant of flowers.

The nurse stopped Jane and pointed to the side door.

"That's all right, dearie. You should use the side door to get to the visitor parking."

Jane Doe turned around and made a beeline for the side door. She stepped outside and looked back. No security guards followed. Keys were taken out of her pocket, and she raced toward the hospital staff parking lot.

Standing on the edge of the curb, Jane only knew the woman's car was small and white. Nurse Macken called her car a beetle. Jane didn't know what she meant. An intern stopped to help.

"My beetle."

The intern looked over the lot.

"There's a beetle in the corner." He pointed, and she saw a small car.

"Just use the clicker when you get there. The car should beep, and the lights should go on. You have a smart key."

The intern walked away.

Jane meandered over to the car and touched the driver's door. No one was looking. She pushed the button on the key. Sure enough, the doors unlocked, the lights flicked, and the horn honked. She never saw such a thing. The heavy flowerpot was put in the backseat.

When she sat in the car, she buckled her seatbelt and looked at the key and the lock. She pushed the lock once and twice. The car didn't start. She repeated the motion. The car still wouldn't start.

Jane sat there and finally opened the glove compartment. She took out the car manual and found the page she was looking for. She saw the pictures and read about how to start the beetle. Stepping on the brake, she punched the start button twice. The engine purred.

She decided to drive home or close to home. Nostalgia hit her when she drove down Wabasha's main street. The car was parked near the post office. Everything looked different. Jane walked down to a small park where a new eagle museum resided.

Then she saw the monstrous structure. There was a new bridge across the Mississippi River. She didn't know how to cross this bridge. Her mind remembered the old crooked bridge with a sharp turn. She read the plaque near the water's edge.

"The new bridge was built in 1988. The date must be wrong. Why can't I remember this bridge? Parts of my memory are gone."

Jane also was hungry. She went back to her stolen car. Inside the center console was a small coin purse and paper money. She counted the amount. The funds were five dollars.

Jane figured how to cross the new bridge and drove to her old home. Different people were living in the house. She drove to her father's girlfriend's place. The garage door was up, so she knew the girlfriend was out shopping.

Her father stored some of her boxes in the garage. Jane found the boxes. She took her high school yearbook and found her birth certificate. There were some old rubber boots she also took.

An idea hit her of where she could live.

"Mrs. Abrams has a house in the country. Won't she be excited to see one of her students again? Too bad she dropped me from the cheerleading squad. That was a huge error on her part. People must pay for their mistakes."

THE PRESENT

15 BODY PARTS FOUND

Renee Kendra was drinking her cup of coffee and looking at the field across from the cabin. She felt the train's vibration before she heard the huge long machine. She watched as the arm came down blocking the roadway on both sides. The lights started flashing. She waited for the train horn. They were getting used to the train sounds.

That is when she saw the police vehicles stop with a large flatbed truck with a small digger. Renee called her husband over to watch the railroad crossing scene.

"I wonder what's happening that the cops need a digger?"

Renee looked at her husband. She worked on this book for months and talked with him every day about the interviews.

"Dead body to match the arm. They've found someone on the beach where the tree fell," said Renee with excitement.

Her husband watched her eyes. "I'm not going to bet on this one. I always lose. What arm are we talking about?"

She smiled. "I went to the store to get some lemon juice. An old man told me somebody walking the beach with his dog found a lower arm bone. The man who found the bone thought they were from a female. He was a biologist from the Twin Cities who has a cabin near the lake. From the length of the bone, the man calculated the female was tall. Amber was short."

"Arm bone? This is unreal. Where's the rest of the body?"

Renee thought for a minute.

"Who knows? The rest of the body could be in the same place or could have drifted downstream. I also overheard a farmer was telling people in town that his kid saw four tires through the muck in his swamp. The farmer didn't believe his child. It's either on the beach or in a swamp. Maybe the rest of the body is in the car trunk."

Her husband frowned his disbelief.

"Now that scene you just described is morbid. Where do you get your ideas? No, don't tell me. Did the sheriff check the tires in the swamp out?"

She couldn't be sure if the sheriff knew about the swamp. "I imagine they will get to the strange tires after they've finished at the beach."

"Shouldn't you go down there to investigate?"

Renee shook her head.

"No, I'm way ahead of the police. You might call my ideas intuition or preconceived knowledge about the way people can kill each other. I wish that I were psychic. My job would be so much easier. There's no need to wait for the results. I think that I'll start painting."

Her husband watched as his wife went into the blue bedroom where she brought her small portable easel out from the closet. After an hour, she was still staring at the white canvas board. He stepped into the room.

"Painter's block?"

He saw her mixture of gray acrylic. The acrylic was the first layer before the drawing and oil paint. Next to her were some photographs of billowing sails. He picked up one with the evening sun.

"I like this picture."

She looked at the photograph. The pictures were aids. She would create her pretty sails and the water.

"Yes, I think an evening picture would work. There's the calming effect of the sun disappearing. The sails should be filled with water racing past."

He knew Renee needed to put dead bodies aside for a while. He was glad she was taking a break. If there was a body, the area would be cordoned off for the investigators. The fishermen would have to put their boats in the water somewhere else. Life would maneuver around the mess.

He watched as she took a large brush and began applying paint. She moved swiftly with confidence. The dog jumped up on the navy twin convertible couch and took a nap. Her husband left to do the same.

After the paint board was covered in gray, she inspected the canvas.

"Looks good enough to me."

Renee put the brush in the cup of water and swirled the bristles. The clean water turned to a murky color. She wiped the brush on a paper towel until it was empty of fluid.

Doug came back. He couldn't sleep. "Why do you put gray acrylic on the paint board?"

"Because the white might show through where I don't want. This way the oil paint will cover the board much better."

He shook his head. She did make sense.

His wife looked out the window toward the train tracks. She saw a firetruck and coroner's car drive over the tracks. The beach was getting a lot of attention.

Renee went into the small kitchen and looked at the whole chicken on the countertop. The dog was by her side.

"Come on, digger dog, let's pick some green beans."

She and the dog disappeared behind the garden gate. The neighbor's chickens came closer. They were orange and white. "Either the mom, dad, or boys are home, and they let the chickens out."

The dog kept sniffing at the garden plants, ignoring the strange birds. He knew some distance was required for chickens. Ten feet was better than two.

Taking the pan of beans, a few tomatoes, and some aster flowers, they went back inside the cabin to prepare supper.

As soon as she and the dog got inside, a cloud emptied, and the rain poured for a straight hour.

Renee could imagine the scene at the beach. She was sure they put a tent over the spot. "I would say they cut things a little too close."

She took her knife and chopped one side of the leg into pieces.

"I should buy one of those cleaver knife things. Whack! Half a chicken appears as if by magic. Another hit and we have a quarter."

The dog ran back to the safety of the couch. Her husband hollered.

"I heard your comments. No knife cleavers. You're scaring me and the dog."

"I'm a certified chef, you know."

He laughed. "Yes, and the education was expensive."

Once the chicken pieces were washed and patted dry, she took the breadcrumbs and flour out. There were a few eggs in this refrigerator, so she didn't need to get the box from the garage refrigerator.

After breading the pieces, she put them on a grated tray. The green beans were washed and ready. Two golden potatoes were washed and left on the counter.

Renee couldn't stand it. "I'm going to take the truck and check for mail."

Her husband awoke. "What's for dinner?"

"The chicken pieces are ready for frying. We'll microwave the potatoes. The beans will take ten minutes in the pot on the stove."

"Do you want me to start the chicken?"

Renee hesitated. She knew the road would be blocked. "Okay, but I'm leaving the dog."

Her husband frowned. The dog was already dancing. He knew the word, *mail*.

Renee looked at her dog's pleading eyes.

"Now, you are brave. You can go with me."

Renee drove out the garage, stopped to get the mail from the dilapidated mailbox, and drove to the stop sign. She talked to the dog.

"You convince the owner to buy a new mailbox, and I'll buy your dog biscuits. He doesn't care if our mail is wet. Well, here goes nothing."

The police stopped her right before the left turn that went to cabins on East Lake Drive and the Y-Campgrounds.

"Sorry, Mrs. Kendra, only the local people are allowed through this area."

The officer pointed out the direction that she should maneuver her vehicle. Renee complied. She saw enough to know the parking area by the boat ramp was covered in vehicles belonging to various police departments. The firetruck was sitting on one side of the road. The empty flatbed and truck were behind the firetruck.

"We knew this was going to happen. I doubt they will find any evidence."

The dog looked out the window content to be going for a drive, albeit a short one.

When she returned home, the smell of cooked chicken made her feel happy that she was back, and that her husband liked to cook. He was a good and dutiful husband.

She saw that he poured her a glass of white wine. Renee didn't speak.

"Well?"

"Thank you, sweetie! The place is an absolute mess. There are vehicles all over the road and the parking lot."

She took a fork and tried one of the cooked pieces of chicken from the plate.

"Hot, but very good." Renee cut another piece and blew it cool. She fed the piece to the dog.

"Hey, no feeding the dog, especially the thigh meat. I like thighs."

He gave her a quick kiss. "You thighs are pretty nice, too."

She kissed him to show her appreciation. Renee took her wine and sat down on the black leather couch to wait until dinner was ready.

16 TRAVELING HOME

The Kendra's stayed until November before traveling back to Arizona. They were delighted with the owner of the lot next to the boat ramp giving them access to information. The newspaper would carry the story shortly. The DNA test showed the lower arm bone didn't belong to Amber Wood.

Renee called Mrs. Wood to give her an update on the bone discovery. She took the news in stride.

"I have an old friend of Amber's who contacted me. I talked to her about your book on Amber. I told her that you were collecting important biographical information. She told me that her family traveled to Phoenix for some golf tournaments. Trixie would like to meet with you for lunch."

"I would love to talk with her. Her name is still on my list for the book."

Mrs. Wood hesitated.

"Her maiden name was Moran. She wanted to know if you could be discreet and not use her real name in your book?"

"Of course, I will be changing most of the names to protect people's identities."

Mrs. Wood was going to hang up but decided there was one more item.

"Please do not tell Alec Rivers about Trixie."

It was Renee's turn to be surprised.

"I will honor your request."

Mrs. Wood explained, "Trixie never trusted nor liked Alec. She only saw him once at a game which was enough. His behavior was over the top. She warned Amber to stay away. Trixie, of course, doesn't trust too many people. She feels a person's vibrations. Amber told me once that if she ever had a sister, that person would be Trixie. They somehow became remarkably close in a short time."

Mrs. Wood gave her Trixie's phone number. Renee hung up her cell phone.

She thought about Trixie's request. Renee sent a text to Alec before she left Wisconsin. There was little information that was shared with him that he couldn't read in a newspaper. He would have to wait for her book to read the story.

Renee hadn't found any other information regarding the disappearance. Nobody seemed to know what happened to Amber.

Her mother had previously explained that Amber left at six in the evening and the sheriff saw her car around ten minutes after nine that same evening. When her parents reported her missing, the sheriff checked the license plate on the main street. Her car was empty inside other than car registration and insurance card in the glove compartment. There was some sand on the floor. Sand on the floor was not unusual in the town of Pepin. The stuff was everywhere.

Renee looked at her handwritten notes hoping to extract more.

"Trixie might be the psychic that I need. No one seems to know about this woman's disappearance. Amber kept their relationship secret. I wonder why? The protection of a best-loved friend would be my guess. I'm glad Amber found such a valuable friend. I will be interested in what she has to say."

Renee didn't put Trixie's name on her computer and used only her initials in her notes.

"Some names are better left in a person's head."

She keyed the phone number in her phone and put Trixie under the heading of hair-colorist. That way, no one would call the number.

Their trip back to Arizona took four days. Renee and her husband were glad to be back in warmth and sunshine. There was no garden to attend to, just her orchids and herb plants. Also, there was a little amount of rain.

In the morning she watched the tribe of quail coming down the side of their yard to get a drink out of the round cement birdbath top. There was a timer that fed the water into the bowl. The tiny birds splashed and took baths. On occasion, she would see the red cardinal male before the female. The cardinals quickly took their drink and flew away.

Renee immediately stepped outside the back patio and walked past the pool. She unhooked the hummingbird feeder and went inside.

She washed the container, filled the glass with the correct amount of sugar water, went to the large bush, and re-hooked the feeder.

Within five minutes she saw the little hummingbird buzz around the female woodpecker. The hummingbird would have to wait her turn. Renee noticed the woodpecker was hogging the feeder. She stepped back outside. The woodpecker flew away, and she talked to the hummingbird while it drank the sweet juice.

"Playing fair is important to survival." She figured Trixie played fair.

17 CALL TO MRS. ABRAMS

She dug out the phone number and dialed it.

Mrs. Abrams immediately answered her phone, Renee introduced herself.

"I didn't know you were married." She asked her about Amber Wood which was the real reason for her call.

Mrs. Abrams was delighted to talk to someone. "She was such a lovely girl and talented, too. Star Malone's father was the band instructor. He let his daughter have the key to the band room to play her flute. One day I heard the flute playing and thought nothing about the music."

"I also didn't know Star played an instrument," said Renee.

"Yes, well, this time the playing was exceptional. Next, I heard the piano. The piece was a difficult one. There was also the violin solo. The music made me want to weep."

"Whoever was playing the instruments was a gifted musician?"

"Exactly! I knew the person was not Star. I went to the band leader's office when the drums started playing. Star's father quickly rose and rushed from the room. The drums were his, and he was very protective of his equipment."

"Star's father was upset his daughter let someone play his drums?" commented Renee.

"I heard laughter as I approached the band room. They were talking about playing a concert for the school program. Amber was holding the drummer sticks. She was the musician playing the instruments. Oh, yes. To answer your question, I was married. Our life together was way too short."

Renee smiled. She needed to ask Mrs. Abrams the question she asked the others.

"Do you know of anyone who might have wanted to hurt Amber or scare her enough to disappear?"

Mrs. Abrams paused. "There is one person whom I shouldn't mention. My life changed for the better ten years ago when I married my husband. He's gone now. He did build a new two-car garage and a heated workshop. I just sold most of his woodworking equipment. There's a small microwave, refrigerator, and couch still in the room. My neighbor thinks I should rent the room out."

Renee knew Mrs. Abrams was wandering in her thoughts.

"I didn't catch the name of the person you might think would harm Amber Wood?"

"Belinda Cummings would be my guess. She was off her rocker most of the time. She was normal one day, and the next day she was different. She acted like a stranger."

Renee wondered about a schizophrenic personality disorder.

"Can you tell me briefly why you think Belinda was unstable?"

Mrs. Abrams paused and answered her door.

"My post lady dropped off my medicine. My heart has been acting up lately. Let me think. It was her sophomore year after Belinda's mother died. She was in biology class. They were supposed to dissect a frog. All the kids wore aprons, and they were supposed to put the parts on a small tray. The biology teacher gave Belinda her apron, tray, and a dead frog. He turned to talk to another male student. He hadn't yet given Belinda the small knife."

Mrs. Abrams took a drink of water and continued.

"Belinda looked at the almost white frog which probably resembled dead fish. She took a small hammer out of her pocket and smashed the poor frog repeatedly. She picked up the decimated pieces and put them on her tray. She wrote in black magic marker the words, *Fixed You, Mother sucker.* The tray was handed to her teacher. The biology teacher decided, quite wisely, not to give her the small knife. He told her she passed and led her to the principal's office where her father came to get her. She was out of school for a week after this incident."

Renee's head was spinning on the last sentence. "There were more incidents?"

Mrs. Abrams continued, "A biology experiment that exploded. Also, one time was the needles all over herself, and another time she squeezed herself inside the gym locker. We had to have her father come to pry her out. Again, she missed school."

Renee was a little disturbed by the events. It was clear there was something wrong. The incidents were more than acting out.

"Was that all the incidents?"

"No, she put some cane poles around her car in the parking lot and strung nets. Next, she hung dead carp on the nets. Again, her father came to get her. She was out of school for three weeks. There was a gun incident. She wasn't on school property. Belinda stood in the middle of the road twirling the gun. She told the police she was practicing baton twirling. The gun wasn't loaded. She almost didn't finish tenth grade. They let her do some classwork at home during the summer. The principal told her father if there was one more incident, she would be out of school permanent. Belinda did settle down."

"Thank you, Mrs. Abrams, for talking with me. I would like to meet with you when we return to Wisconsin."

Mrs. Abrams laughed. "I'll be here. I want to give you one of the little birds that my husband carved. The birds are signed. I'll find one when I get out to the shop and mail you the package. Give me a few weeks."

"I would love to own such a piece. I appreciate your kindness. I'm partial to birds."

18 RESEARCH THE WOOD COUPLE

Renee knew she was reading the files on Amber's parents, Connie, and Cyrus Wood. Cyrus was a highly experienced chemical engineer who worked for a large company. They had offices all over the world. The office that interested her was Seattle, Washington. Per a call to his old office, he traveled to the city the most.

It appeared this was the location the two people met before they were married and lived in Minneapolis later. Connie was a member of a symphony orchestra and played percussion. Cyrus liked to attend concerts whenever he was in Seattle. The two of them married in Vancouver.

Renee read the marriage license. Connie's maiden name was Manus. Renee searched for the name. There were a ton of hits. She tried C. Manus and found a Cara Manus who died in a rock-climbing accident in Washington state. Cara had a daughter, but that was all Renee could find out.

She wondered if Connie was related to Cara. The relationship seemed a long shot. When she visited Mrs. Wood in her home in Minneapolis, she didn't get to see Mrs. Wood's bedroom. She bet there were a lot of family pictures in the room.

Renee tried to think about how she could find more information without calling Amber's mother.

Amber didn't look anything like her father. Now Renee wondered if Amber was adopted.

"The possibility existed. Adoption papers were hidden most of the time. If they adopted her in a different country, finding the documents would be impossible."

Renee shook her head. She was over-thinking again. The writer in her found ten directions to go. The signs flickered in her head.

"Which path is the right one that will lead me to discovery?" She was in dead space and didn't know how to proceed forward.

"Why is this so important?"

She knew. The book had to be just right.

"I should wait for something to happen. What is that old saying? If you wait long enough, like years and years, all will be revealed. Somehow, whoever said that didn't know what the heck they were talking about. Besides, I don't have years."

She checked the weather in Pepin.

"Snow is in the forecast. Great! Frozen rain is the same as rain."

Renee put her head in her hands.

"Is it too late to join the theatre?"

19 CAR WHEELS

Two boys were walking past the swamp on Rob's old man's farm. They were on their way to the lake to try some ice fishing. There was a tiny shack on the lake thirty feet from shore for them to use.

One of the boys pointed toward the marsh. They saw two tires sticking out of the ice.

"The shape looks like car wheels to me."

The younger boy picked up a rock and threw it at the tires. The rock bounced and came back at them. Both boys ducked.

"Yeah, those are rubber tires. I wonder how they got stuck in the ice?"

The other boy shoved his friend.

"People throw tires away all the time. The dumps are full of the old ones. Sometimes they pile them too high, and they catch fire."

The younger boy noticed the tires were evenly straight. If someone threw them, the tires would be lopsided. "Kool. Maybe we should go back home and get some gasoline to see if the tires will burn."

The older boy scratched his head.

"Nah, I want to go ice fishing. I'm hungry for fried fish. My mom makes fresh-cut French fries when we have fish. She buys sour cream, too. I like sour cream instead of ketchup. Let's burn the tires tomorrow."

The two boys went fishing and caught two small walleye which Rob's mom cooked for their supper. The younger boy was invited for supper and ate fresh fries for the first time.

The next morning, Rob's parents went to town to get groceries. The two boys snuck out to the garage. They grabbed a sled, a can of gasoline, and long wooden matches. At the last minute, they grabbed an old sheet that was torn in half. They knotted the sheet in a few spots.

Trudging back to the frozen tires, they wrapped the sheet around one of the front tires and stretched it out. They knew gasoline would create an explosion, and they needed to stand back at least five feet which were their estimate.

The older boy put some dried grass on the sheet. More dried grass led to the other front tire. Next came the gasoline. At the last minute, he decided to empty the gas container.

"Might as well haul an empty can back home."

The wind picked up a little bit, and they huddled together to light the match and the sheet. They watched as the flame traveled slowly toward the first tire.

"Henri, maybe we miscalculated. We should probably go to the end of the pond on solid ground near the road."

The younger boy approved. "Yeah, that way, if we messed up, we could run home."

They pulled the sled and gas can to the road and turned to watch.

Henri looked at his friend.

"Rob, I don't see any light on the sheet anymore. Maybe the wind blew the flame out."

"No, the sheet is smoking. Smoking means something big is going to hit."

Henri hoped things wouldn't be too big. "The gas might have been too much."

Just then the wind increased, and the flames leaped and lit the sheet on fire. Both boys started running home. They made it to Rob's driveway before the first explosion hit. They dumped the sled and empty gas can in the garage. Both ran into the house to watch.

They looked outside the large glass living room window when the second explosion hit. All the weeds and trees around the pond ignited on fire. The dead leaves on the trees smoked and burned. The wind made the trees sway like dancing snakes. The smoking rubber filled the air with black matter.

In the distance, the boys heard the Stockholm firetruck. The red truck that belonged to the fire marshal arrived. He stepped out of his truck and looked around.

The two boys ducked down out of sight. They peeked again when they saw the red lights from the fire truck. Next, two sheriff's vehicles arrived on the scene.

"I hope my parents don't come home until they put out the fire. I think we'll get blamed."

Henri said, "I've got to go home now. I hear my mom calling."

Rob was surprised. "Don't you want to see the show?"

Henri's head went back and forth like a bobblehead doll. His body was shaking.

"No, no I'm afraid a big monster is in those tires. I could see the tires raise from the window."

Rob watched as a wrecker truck arrived. The firemen helped him hook a chain to the bottom of the metal.

Both boys watched in horror as a rusted, filthy dirty car emerged from the pond. Henri rapidly recovered and ran out the door.

"Bye."

Rob made sure the sled was put back exactly in the same spot. He filled the gas can with some water and tipped the can over. He loosened the cap, so it would look like the gas leaked out. Then he went back into the house and washed his hands twice. He forgot about the soot on his face.

The police rubbed the license plate and wrote down the number. They used a tool to open the doors. There was no one inside. They popped the trunk and rummaged around the junk. The remnants of an old suitcase appeared. The nylon rope, plastic tarp, and two metal anchors were a surprise. They reasoned the anchors helped sink the car.

There was no dead body in the car nor the trunk. The men discussed things. They couldn't figure out how the car arrived to be in an upside-down position all these years. If there hadn't been a fire that started the woods on fire, they never would have found the car that belonged to Belinda Cummings.

Finding Belinda's car raised further questions. Belinda was known in the past to trash her vehicle. The police remembered the dead fish she brought to school. One of the officers threw a dead fish in the grass.

They believed she got tired of this car, too. No one heard from Belinda in a long time. They all believed she went to Madison or Milwaukee. Now, the police weren't so sure. They wondered about the arm bones that no one could figure out. Belinda used to be about five feet eight inches tall.

The police were sure the car belonged to Belinda Cummings. They found her fingerprints and some of the local girls' fingerprints that she went to school with. The prints were found inside on top of the dashboard.

They cleaned out the beer bottles all over the back on the smelly floor mats. The root beer bottles were few. There was a lot of soggy garbage inside the car. They found an old feedbag and some used candles. There was a box of female pads stuffed under a seat. Several pairs of shoes and shorts were on the back seat. A rusted flashlight and a water jug were found in the trunk with tire chains and a jumper cable. There were boxes of cereal and raisins stuck to the inside lid of the car. She must have lived in her car on occasion.

Belinda was also none too neat a person.

The police did find some letters and hanging necklaces inside the vehicle. The ink and postage marks were gone off the paper.

Her father was dead, and there were no relatives. The police contacted the father's old girlfriend who didn't know anything. She told them Belinda was an odd kid. The girlfriend didn't want any piece of junk Belinda previously drove. The door was slammed in their faces.

This information was not updated news to the sheriff or any of the fire department personnel.

The car was sent to the impound lot in Durand in case someone wanted to claim the vehicle in the future. After a year, the car was taken to the dump.

20 A SECOND CAR

A year and a half later during the spring, Henri passed the swamp when he heard a car stop.

He hid in the tall weeds and the wild lilies in the ditch. Henri took his tiny telescope from his back pocket. The toy was better than nothing. He watched. An old woman got out of the light-colored car, removed the license plate, and shoved the small car into the water.

"She looks old, but she has lots of muscle."

Henri was so scared. He didn't move. He put his telescope away. The lens was scratched. His body started shaking again. He grabbed butterscotch out of his pocket, popped the disk in his mouth, and shut his eyes. Finally, he peered out and saw the car submerge into the water. He couldn't believe there was a second car in the pond.

"Nobody is going to believe me, not even Rob."

Now he had to pee. He was too scared to go in the weeds for fear a snake would jump out of the pond to make room for the car.

"Snakes can jump how many feet? I know it must be a big number. This is my unluckiest day ever."

Henri listened. He didn't hear anything. He stood up and saw the woman in the distance disappear in a dip in the road. He ran as fast as he could to Rob's house.

Rob opened the door and watched his friend run to the bathroom. When Henri emerged, he collapsed on the couch. Rob faithfully brought him a glass of cold water.

Henri stuttered, "There's another car in the swampy and deep pond."

Rob couldn't believe the words. Henri only stuttered when he was scared walking the dark gravel roads during Halloween night. He was used to Henri's weaknesses.

"No, there isn't a car there. Last time, I was the one who got into trouble. My face was full of soot. You should have warned me. My parents were mad at me for a month. Now, repeat after me, there is nothing in the water."

Henri wasn't buying the falsehood.

"There is nothing in the water, except maybe an alien car and a few dead mosquitoes."

Rob took away the water glass. "Go home, Henri. You are delusional today or half-crazy. There isn't a car. If you say there's something in the pond one more time, I won't know you."

Henri's shoulders drooped. His friend didn't believe him. He walked slowly home and kept looking over his shoulder.

"I'm not crazy halfway. The woman is an alien. Aliens don't exist. Everybody tells you. What do they know? They don't live in the country. Country roads at night are where you don't want to be. Also, aliens are smart, and they avoid large cities. If they must go to the city, they disguise themselves. She was wearing baggy sweatpants stuff. Half the women in town wear the gear. This alien blends in. She has cunning."

Once at home, Henri's paranoia lessened. His curiosity took over in the safety of his bedroom. He picked up a magazine and was strumming through the pages. He saw a picture of the car. There was a story about some hippies. They painted the body with flowers, but the outside body was the same as the alien's car.

Henri ripped the picture out of the magazine and took a thumbtack. He pushed the tack into the photo and secured it to the corkboard.

"I'm not an idiot. I saw this type of car. Someday the car will surface. Then my friend will believe me."

Henri kept looking for the woman in town when his mom made him go shopping with her. One time he thought he saw her with a different car getting gas. The car looked exactly like Mrs. Abrams' vehicle. He knew Mrs. Abrams didn't drive much anymore. Henri ducked down.

Henri wondered if he could get Rob to walk to Mrs. Abrams' house. He wanted to make sure her car was in the garage. Besides, Mrs. Abrams let them pick apples off her trees in the summer. Henri liked apple pie as did Rob.

Every night before Henri went to bed, he looked at the flower car on his bulletin board. It suddenly occurred to him the car might have been stolen.

"The woman needed to dump the car where no one would find it. She must have seen the news coverage of the other car to know this deep pond existed. If she saw the news, she must live in the area.

But then she might have cable or a dish or something to get more channels on the television."

Henri walked back to the pond with his fishing pole. The pole was one of those cane affairs with a line and a single hook. He sat down his can of earthworms freshly dug this morning.

Henri threw out his line. The worm fell off. A frog jumped into the pond and ate the worm. He tried two worms this time. One worm fell off, and the other one stayed on.

Rob saw Henri from the window.

"What is Henri doing? There's no fish in that pond. He's trying to get my goat for not believing him. I'm not going to look anymore."

Rob picked up a new comic book. After five minutes, he gave up, put the book in his back pocket, and sauntered outside. He slowly walked down the road with two cans of cola.

"Hi, Henri, are you trying to catch a frog? We could use a frog to go fishing at the lake. I have a new bike that goes faster. My mom was sore at my dad, so she bought me a bike."

Henri was envious. "I'd like a new bike. My one tire is low. The air pump isn't working. I've got to wait until my dad can fix the tire."

Rob shared more information now that Henri was talking to him again. "Bummer. You could use my tire pump. Oh, my bike has a metal-type bar in the back, so someone could ride with me. There are even baskets to put the fish in."

"Wow, I'd like to see your new bike. Maybe we can use my worms to go fishing."

Henri threw out his line one last time while he waited for Rob to decide on the bike ride.

The hook caught on something. Henri tugged at the line to no avail. He couldn't dislodge the hook. He hated cutting the line.

"Here, let me try." Rob walked around the pond, and the hook gave way.

"See, the line is free."

The two boys walked back to Rob's house to check out his new bike and find the air pump.

"I believe you about the lady pushing the car in the pond," confessed Rob.

"Really?"

"Yeah, it makes perfect sense. The old woman didn't own the car. The car belonged to her ex-husband. She hated the darn thing and got rid of the ugly piece of crap metal. If she took the car to the dump, they charge a fee."

Henri laughed. "I thought the lady was an alien."

The older boy looked at his younger friend. It was time to explain the human species.

"My dad told me women get weird when a boyfriend drops them, or they get divorced. He was trying to warn me to stay away from girls. We can call the woman who dumped the car the *she-alien*. It is odd that a year and a half later we have another car in the pond. For now, we keep the car a secret."

121

"Okay," agreed Henri. He was cool with the idea. A pact was made. Henri thought about the photo on his board.

"When we get older, we might want to pull the car out. I bet we can repaint the outside."

Rob thought about it. "VIN is important. We can't change the numbers because that would be illegal. Maybe we could buy the car real cheap and work on it when we're fifteen."

"You're smart. We have a deal." Suddenly, Henri remembered. "My dad tells me real stuff sometimes. I think I saw the woman in town at the gas station in Mrs. Abrams' car."

Rob couldn't believe the ongoing story. He wished he hadn't named the woman.

"Now, Henri, don't go back to crazy thinking. There is no car in the water, and you saw nothing."

Rob was right. Henri should forget about the woman. She might be a real person. She sounded dangerous and looked weird. He saw the look on the woman's face. It wasn't nice.

"I saw nothing."

21 MRS. ABRAMS' VISITOR

Mrs. Abrams thought she heard a noise coming from her husband's shop.

"Did I see someone drive in the yard? Where are my glasses?" She grabbed them and put the eyewear into her pocket. Mrs. Abrams rarely wore the things.

She looked out her side window, and there was only gravel in her driveway.

"I am imagining things. I can't even remember if I locked the outside shop door. Well, it's too dark to look now. I'll check on things in the morning when there is light. I must get Renee Kendra a little bird. It's the least I can do for nice neighbors."

The next morning, Mrs. Abrams looked in the shop. Nothing was disturbed. She selected a light wood bird and smiled.

"This bird looks like it belongs in Arizona. My husband did a good job on this little guy."

She hugged the small item and placed the object in her other pocket. She punched in the code to open the garage where her car was kept. The car stood in its place. Mrs. Abram didn't check the other garage. There was no need. The garages were separated by a firewall. Her husband thought about renting the space to a boater and changed his mind. The second garage was empty the last time she looked.

Mrs. Abram went back into her home to make breakfast. She took out two patties of hamburger from the freezer and placed the patties in a deep dish to thaw.

Next, she got out a pie plate, flour, salt, butter, and a measuring cup of water. She made her pie crust, formed the dough into a large mound, and placed the mound in plastic wrap. The dough was put in the refrigerator.

Mrs. Abrams remembered the little bird. She found a small box, wrapped the wood bird in tissue, and taped the box shut. She wrote Renee's address on the outside. Digging into her money jar, she placed two dollars in an envelope for her mail lady. The box and envelope were put in her mailbox on the porch.

She would make an apple pie this afternoon. Her heart pills were on the counter. Mrs. Abrams would take a pill later. For now, she was headed to the door of the root cellar to get the canned jar of apples before making her toast.

She held onto the railing and walked down the steps. At the bottom, her heart started hurting. She sat down on a wooden chair and scanned the tiny room. Her sweater was upstairs. The room was cold.

Mrs. Abrams selected the jar of apples and turned. In the doorway, she saw a ghost.

"Belinda Cummings, is that you?"

The ghost turned into a human. "Hello, Mrs. Abrams, how nice to see you again. Here, let me take the jar of apples from you. We don't want you to drop good apples."

Mrs. Abrams complied.

"The police found your car in the old Jones pond. They will want to hear from you. My phone is upstairs."

Belinda looked around the cellar. "No, I don't want to talk to the sheriff. I still don't remember things. My mind remembered you and this house. You didn't hate me when I was a cheerleader. I understand you follow the rules. No pushing. I pushed and was dropped from the team."

Mrs. Abrams's breathing improved.

"Let's get back upstairs. I need a cup of hot tea with toast, and it's chilly down here. Rules are important. I'm glad you understand."

Belinda turned and went upstairs with the apples. She turned the sink tap on and filled the tea kettle. Lighting the stove, she placed the pot on top of the stove. Belinda sat down while Mrs. Abrams found the cups and tea bags.

The old woman cut some lemon slices and put them on a plate. Two slices of bread were put in the toaster.

Belinda picked one of the pieces of toast.

"I forgot that you made your bread. This one tastes better than the packaged bread."

Mrs. Abrams brought over the kettle and filled the cups. Each woman made their tea.

"I forgot to ask if you need sugar?"

"No."

The two women sat for some time. Finally, Belinda broke the silence.

"I need a place to stay and possibly a ride to work and back. The tiny hamburger place has a sign. They need a waitress. After three months, I'll have enough money to move along."

"Where would you stay?"

Belinda swallowed her last bite of the thick toast. "I saw a workshop. There appears to be a heater, small refrigerator, microwave, and couch. I just need blankets and towels. Maybe a few dishes and pans. Food from your cellar would be fine. Can you help me?"

Mrs. Abrams was a kind woman, and she knew her place on this earth was to be neighborly.

"I can let you drive my car back and forth to work. You can stay for three months but no longer. If you are still here, I will call Sheriff Edwards, and there is to be no funny stuff."

Belinda won over the old woman. "I will be fine. If I go nuts, you can use that gun I saw in your pantry."

Mrs. Abrams was startled Belinda knew about her gun. She stirred her tea a little longer than necessary. She noticed the fake arm. "Can you tell me where you have been all these years?"

Belinda couldn't hide the fact she was missing an arm. "There was a large building with old people and nurses. Occasionally the doctors showed up or the psychiatrists."

In disbelief, Mrs. Abrams commented, "You were in a nursing home?"

Belinda nodded. There was no reason to divulge any more regarding the places she lived. "I was ill for a long time. They gave me pills. I'm better. I have some flowers in a pot. They let me have the flowers as a goodbye present. People were nice to me."

Mrs. Abrams wasn't so sure. People weren't usually nice to Belinda after a day or two. She hesitated briefly.

"I'm glad they were friendly. We're having hamburgers, corn, baked potato, and apple pie for supper. I'll get you some bedding and towels. There's some frozen bread in the freezer and jelly. Later, we'll pack you some groceries. The dishes and pots are in the shop under the sink."

Mrs. Abrams reached for a jar in the cupboard and pulled out two twenty-dollar bills.

"This should help get you started. Now, take my car and fill out the job application in town. You can put down my address and phone as a reference."

She handed Belinda her car keys. The woman disappeared.

"Someone in town must have noticed Belinda Cummings was here. I'll be safe."

After the woman left, Mrs. Abrams took her heart pill and sat down. For the first time in a long time, she was afraid. She sent up a silent prayer.

"I might be joining you sooner than planned, dear."

22 MRS. ABRAMS' HOUSE

The two boys sat on their bicycles on the wet gravel road. Three months passed since Mrs. Abrams saw her visitor arrive. They watched as the sheriff and other law enforcement walked the perimeter of the property.

Henri said, "I should have stopped for a visit. I was going to visit her, but I got busy with school and other stuff."

Rob felt guilty, too. "My dad told me the post lady saw her sitting in her rocker chair with a large red spot on her chest. She thought the red spot was a flower until the post lady got closer. The red was from a bullet."

Henri's eyes clouded. "Who would want to kill nice Mrs. Abrams? You said a bullet, not a shell?"

Rob frowned. He was thinking.

"A bullet is found in revolvers. The gun wasn't a deer rifle. Remember the white car you saw go into the pond?"

Henri was distracted from the red spot. "Yeah, I think the white car is still there."

Rob speculated, "What if the murderer owned the white car?"

Henri looked scared and wondered. "Are we in trouble again?"

The coroner's vehicle took the body away. Henri started crying, and then he pedaled fast toward his home. Rob stayed and continued to watch. The sheriff came over to talk to Rob.

"Did you boys see anything strange around Mrs. Abrams' house in the last two or three months?"

"No, sir. Both of us were busy and weren't in the neighborhood. We did see something strange near our pond."

The sheriff remembered pulling Belinda's car out.

"The police found a car in the pond. It's gone to the dump. There's no need to worry anymore."

Rob hesitated. He hated being the older person at this juncture. He wished he were following his friend home.

"Not that car. There's another car that went into the pond. Henri saw a woman dressed in sweatpants push a white car in. I think the time was about three months ago. He was too frightened to tell anyone. He showed me a picture from a magazine of what the car might look like. The picture was a flowered version of the beetle. The woman seemed to scare him; you know like she was an alien. Henri sees strange stuff and has bad dreams. He's younger than me. I thought the car idea was a mirage. That's why I didn't say anything."

The sheriff wasn't listening until he heard the word beetle.

"The woman scared Henri. That's mighty interesting. Thanks, Rob, we'll check the pond. Mrs. Abrams was ill. She couldn't see very well, and walking was difficult. Her ticker was acting up, and she could have died of natural causes at any time per her doctor."

Rob didn't know what to say. The sheriff continued.

"Tell your dad Mrs. Abrams was shot with a handgun. She owned a nine-millimeter which is missing. Someone shot her with her gun. One bullet to her heart. We're going to catch this murderer. You go along home now. There's nothing you can do here except be catching a nasty cold. She's with her husband in a peaceful place, and he'll take loving care of her."

Rob was glad he talked with the sheriff. His words mattered. The sheriff knew how to catch criminals. The car would be hauled away. He reflected Mrs. Abrams was probably happier now.

"Yes, sir."

Rob rode slowly home. He would ask his mom if he could bring some flowers and put them on Mrs. Abrams' porch. He would need to tell Henri they couldn't have the white car. The police would come to get the vehicle out of their swamp for evidence.

DANGER IN THE AIR

23 THE NURSE'S BEETLE

The FBI was called into Mrs. Abrams' murder because the nurse's white beetle car was found in a different state.

The investigators found Jane Doe an interesting suspect. They talked with the staff at the nursing home in Rochester and the hospital in Wabasha. Her being transferred to a mental hospital was noted.

They showed the investigators the one picture they took when Jane Doe was first brought to them. The woman looked asleep. They wondered how she could even see or walk, much less drive a car. They worried she might have an accomplice.

The investigators learned her lower left arm which was amputated appeared to have been stolen from the hospital. How the arm ended up on the beach was hard to explain. They felt sure her arm was the part found on Deer Island in Wisconsin.

They were looking for a very disturbed person by the name of Belinda Cummings and possibly a helper. An alert went out for her arrest in all the nearby Midwest states. Her name and high school graduation picture was splashed over the news channels in the evening and hit the newspapers as far north as Duluth.

Alec Rivers sat in his elegant house in Minneapolis with his wife and two children. He was reading the article while eating his eggs. The picture revolted him. He put the newspaper in his briefcase.

His wife handed him his filled coffee mug. He didn't take the mug. She placed the to-go mug on the table.

Usually, her husband rushed off to work in his tall office building. She packed her two children's lunch boxes and escorted her girls to the bus stop. She waited until the bus released its brake and left their neighborhood.

Alec was tapping his knife on his plate. He was angry at himself. It was his fault Belinda was still alive. He should have left her on the beach years ago. He remembered the bad scene. His wife knew something was wrong.

"Giselle, there's been a murder in Pepin. The person was a retired teacher. The police believe the murderer was a former student. Unfortunately, I knew this student twenty years ago. The police may have some questions for me."

Gisele leaned against the counter. Her arms were crossed in a defensive move. "I don't understand. How do you know these people?"

He didn't answer her question. The story would be too long.

"I'm not worried about the police. I handle cops all the time. This student is violent. She may be reaching out to people in her past. The police think she doesn't have much money and will be looking for a place to live. She could come here and hurt you or the kids."

Gisele uncrossed her arms. She looked around her brightly lit kitchen. "We should go for a visit to my parent's ranch in Wyoming."

"I think that is an excellent idea. You can easily switch schools for our girls."

Gisele needed clarification as she was still stunned, "Do you think we will be gone that long?"

"Yes. She's hidden for twenty years and avoided detection. The cunning in this person is very high. She isn't to be underestimated. We will take all necessary precautions. I will stay here and continue working."

His wife was going to object until she saw his determined face. Nothing would sway him. She stood up.

"Does this have anything to do with your website and the Amber person?"

There was no response from Alec. She knew the name hit a sore spot.

"I'll start packing our suitcases. Will you drive us to Wyoming? I hate to drive. There might be a hailstorm."

He sighed. "Let me make a call." Alec disappeared and called his office. He found his wife in their bedroom. "I have to be back to work in five days or six. I'll drive you there and fly back."

He went to his home office and sat in his chair. He was worried Belinda was near his turf. "How dare she come here? She didn't learn her lesson. Or she doesn't remember. I'm always right. This time, I'm wrong. She remembers."

He took a rubber ball on his desk and bounced it softly against the wood. He stopped and squeezed the ball as hard as he could. His brain was rapidly firing about how he could rig his house. Alec was sure Belinda would come to his home eventually. He drove home.

Alec went to the safe on his wall and took out his revolver. He put bullets in the gun and put the gun in his desk drawer. He locked the drawer for now. Next, he went to his case of deer rifles. He took one out and looked through the scope. Opening the lower drawer, he checked the number of boxes of shells.

"There should be enough. I need to buy some metal supports for the rifles and buy another revolver for work."

He input the list of items required into his phone. Alec went to the master bedroom to pack a light bag.

Gisele held the two girl's suitcases, and the backpacks were ready. Alec went down to his garage and put the items in their large SUV vehicle. They would pick up the girls at noon. His wife already called the school and her parents in Wyoming.

Alec made his airline and car reservations. His wife carried her suitcase and computer bag to the kitchen. He took her items to the car along with his briefcase.

When he came back to the kitchen, there was a large garbage bag of items from the refrigerator. He took that out to their garbage receptacle.

"You'll need to buy groceries when you get home."

Alec didn't care about cooking. "I'll probably eat out."

She went to the computer on the wall and checked the doors and windows.

"Things look locked except the door to our garage. We're ready to go."

Gisele went to the vehicle and climbed inside. Alec climbed in the car and drove out of the garage. He stopped and used his phone to lock the last doors. He notified the security company they would be gone for six days. Alec would let them know when he returned.

They both watched as their eight and ten-year-old girls climbed into the car. They were happy to be going to Wyoming. His wife's parents owned cats, dogs, and horses. There were two goats for more entertainment.

Alec knew his wife would be more comfortable with her parents than in his house. Lately, his wife was moody. Being in Wyoming, she could visit with her old friends while Alec took care of their problem.

They stopped at a chicken fast food place for lunch. His wife and girls ran inside the restaurant. He talked to himself.

"I'll have to make sure the scene looks like an intruder entered our home."

Alec went inside the restaurant to eat. They would need to get gas and some treats to eat along the way. He knew that he was doing the right thing. His family wasn't part of his past.

Alec thought about Amber for a few minutes while his wife and daughters went to the restroom. He thought about the sweet teenager he knew every day of his life. Not knowing what happened was torture. His life revolved around finding Amber and his family. Alec was married to both in a way. He rationalized the killing of Belinda would be for the disappearance of Amber.

"She needs to pay."

He opened his paper bag and found his sandwich marked no mayonnaise. Alec took the coffee from the table. He undid the lid, and the hot aroma of coffee filled his nostrils. His wife already poured in the cream.

"Belinda Cummings will pay. I will fight her until my dying breath."

24 BELINDA IN MINNEAPOLIS

Mrs. Abrams' car was left at a shopping center parking lot. There were many restaurants in the area and cars were coming and going all the time. The lot was chosen because the street was on a major bus route.

Belinda looked at her map and the address of the tall tower building that Alec Rivers worked in. The bus drove past the building. She noticed a coffee shop across the street.

The street sign appeared on her map. She was three blocks from the neighborhood where she was getting off the bus. The neighborhood was small ranch-style houses with two-car garages and basements. She pulled the bus cord. The bus stopped, and Belinda exited. She walked to the house and knocked on the door.

An old man let her into the house and showed her the rental room. There was a separate entrance to the room. Belinda was pleased and gave the man her deposit and first month's rent.

Belinda was pleased when she found Mrs. Abrams' private stashes of money. There were three thousand dollars each in a pair of socks under her dresser drawer. She found another three thousand dollars stuffed in a fruit jar in the cellar. The last three thousand were stuffed inside a macaroni box in the cupboard. In total, she owned over twelve thousand dollars. She had plenty of time to find another job.

"I'll have to steal someone's identification and birth certificate to get a new card."

Belinda wasn't worried. She saw the old man's gun collection when he let her in his part of the house to sign the lease. There was one gun and clip that interested her the most.

Belinda dyed her hair and put in some colored hair tails. Large rimmed glasses changed her looks. She put an old blue jean hat over her head. She walked down the street to a small grocery store on the corner.

A television monitor showed her picture on the screen as a wanted and dangerous person. No one in the store paid any attention to the monitor. A bored teenage girl with nose rings rung up her sale. She paid the unhappy clerk for her groceries and left.

There was a bench outside the store. Belinda sat down and dug the ice cream sandwich out of her bag. She watched the people come and go in the store.

When an elderly woman left the store and walked in the direction Belinda lived, she followed the woman.

The woman was two blocks from Belinda's rental. Belinda took a pen from her pocket and wrote the house number on her paper bag. She didn't see any security company sticker on the woman's door nor the windows.

However, she heard a small barky dog when the woman opened her door. Belinda would have to make sure the woman and dog were out of the house before she broke in.

Belinda shifted her groceries.

"A cart would be nice. I'll ask my rental manager if he has one lying around his garage or basement."

She got lucky when her rental manager went to visit the doctor. Belinda explored his house, garages, and basement. No one was the wiser.

25 CHECK ON ALEC'S OFFICE

Belinda went to the coffee shop and waited. She was sure Alec would walk into the shop to buy coffee. She was mistaken.

Bravely, she crossed the street when the light changed. Belinda stopped and looked behind her. She felt a little creepy like someone was following her.

Once inside the building, she stood looking at the names and floor numbers on the engraved board. Again, she looked around. People were coming and going through the large doors. They were dressed in suits.

She saw the information desk and went over to the attendant. He asked her if she needed any help. Belinda picked up some brochures regarding Minneapolis. There were a few maps.

"Do you have a bag? These brochures are slippery."

The information booth attendant pointed to an eco-friendly bag with advertising. There were several bags on the end. She put her brochures inside and walked to the elevators.

Instead of leaving, she spotted the restrooms and went inside. The place was empty. She did her business and came out. Again, Belinda felt creepy as if she were being watched.

She bit her lip and looked closely at each person. There were too many people to remember all of them.

Belinda stepped into the elevator and punched the button for Alec's floor. She stepped off the elevator with some of the other business workers. She knew her blue jeans and jacket were obvious, as in *unemployed*.

A large department store was two blocks away. Belinda would need to buy a suit and heels to blend in better.

"Maybe a haircut and some lipstick were in order. The women look nice in the building. I look frumpy."

She stopped. This floor contained spaces where a person could hide. She looked behind her again.

"There's a feeling that I'm being watched. I'm usually not this edgy."

Again, she watched people while standing close to the wall. Suddenly, Belinda looked up and saw the security cameras.

"Silly, you are being watched. This building is covered with spies. Valuable information to know. This building won't do for my business."

Belinda stopped at Alec's door. The inside was semi-dark.

"Maybe, he comes in later. I'll ask the receptionist down the hall."

Belinda walked to the receptionist's desk and found out Mr. Rivers was out of the office. The receptionist would give her no other information.

"Would you like to leave your name for Mr. Rivers?"

Belinda wanted to leave her name. She could imagine his face. Shock, surprise, anger, or fear? Fear was what she wanted to see. "No, I'll wait."

She walked back to his office and used her hands to shield the hallway light. Belinda scanned his desk. She saw an in-basket and a pencil holder. There was no stapler. A large nameplate set in wood showed his name. The brass was shiny.

There were copies of diplomas on the walls. There were three chairs and a desk chair. She glanced toward a credenza where she saw a large photograph of his family.

Belinda stopped her ogling and looked around the hall. She still felt like she was being followed.

"No one is following you, Belinda. This is not the time to freak out with all these important businesspeople around."

A security guard stopped. "Do you need some help, ma'am?"

Belinda knew she could get in trouble.

"I was out of breath for a minute. My asthma acts up now and then. My inhaler was left in my living quarters. You probably saw me lean against the glass of that office. It was important to concentrate on my breathing. I do see the water fountain. I'll get a drink, and then I should be fine. Thank you for asking."

The security officer walked away. There was a call on his radio. Belinda took a drink out of the water fountain. The hall was again empty.

She went back to Alec's office and found a different spot to look through the heavy glass. The credenza was closer. She saw a small picture of Amber which surprised her.

In horror, she saw a yellow object. Her mouth became dry, and her eyes bulged. Belinda couldn't believe what she saw. The object made her left arm hurt. Brief flashes of a night on the beach hit her.

Belinda stepped back as if wounded, and her eyes wouldn't focus. She tried to scream, and nothing came out. Her reaction to the object was perfectly understandable. The yellow object was Amber's ball.

She stumbled toward the stairway. Belinda walked quickly down the four floors of stairs. Stepping out onto the street, she gasped for air.

People walked around her frozen body. She needed to get away, but where could she go? She moved in the direction of the department store.

Belinda looked at the lipstick. The hot pink color caught her eye. The sales clerk approached. She pointed to the color and changed her mind to the new dark blue-black look. The clerk disappeared and rung up the purchase.

"The total is fifteen ninety-five."

Belinda's mind raised. Lipstick used to cost two dollars and fifty cents. She took her body bag purse and found a twenty-dollar bill. The sales clerk brought her change and gave her the package.

She asked the clerk where the women's clothing was in the store.

"Take the escalator to the third floor, or there are elevators over to the left."

Belinda took the elevator. Moving through the racks of clothes, she was surprised by the prices. Finally, she found the sale rack. The prices were still too high.

"I need to find a thrift store to buy clothes."

She sat down on a cement bench next to a pretzel vendor. The aroma of bread made her hungry. Belinda bought a large pretzel and cola. She squeezed mustard on the outside and sat down to eat.

Halfway through eating, she looked around. She wasn't used to so many people. Living in Minneapolis would take getting used to. She finished her pretzel and cola. The garbage was thrown in a metal can near the street.

"No use getting a ticket from some fancy lady cop for littering."

Belinda saw the bus and ran. She made the inside step when the door closed. Dropping the coins in the slot, she sat down quickly as the bus driver pulled out into heavy traffic. A few cars honked their horns. The bus driver ignored the angry drivers.

Belinda got off the bus a block from her rental. She walked inside and pulled all the shades on the windows down. She sat in the dark for a long time.

"Alec has Amber's yellow ball. I used to have an amber ball. I gave him a gift, and he left me. He shouldn't have left me."

26 UNSCHEDULED HOUSE TOUR

The bus stopped, and a woman waited for the door to open. She stepped down to the cement curb. This neighborhood was out of her league.

The woman was wearing a cheap suit and blouse from the local thrift store. Her shoes were new that she found on the sale rack for thirty dollars. They were black flats because black went with all colors. This color also made her feet appear smaller.

The time of day was close to sundown. She looked at the streetlights. They weren't on yet in this part of the neighborhood. Belinda kept walking. There was a house that she wanted to see. The address was on a slip of paper in her pocket. Not sure if the person was home or not, she thought it was important to check out.

There were people outside one of the large homes. They appeared to be part of a party. The owner was handing candles to her guests and a small book of matches. The woman handed Belinda a candle and some matches. She asked one of the guests a question.

"Why is everyone outside?"

The woman whispered. "Isn't this fun? I didn't want to come to another stuffy party. It's a good thing the caterers have those flame canisters to heat the food."

Belinda licked her lips.

"There's food?"

"Sure, the food is over there on the large table. The electric company told us the power might be out at

145

least an hour at the minimum. There's a real problem with the box wiring. I guess someone didn't know what they were doing last week on the repair. My theory is you get what you pay for every time."

Belinda's stomach felt sore. "Yes, it's amazing anything gets done. Kids don't do their homework in school. That's where things start to go bad," volunteered Belinda.

She helped herself to a plate of food and took a can of cola with her. The house was down the street. She walked and stopped. Belinda stared at the large front door. She tried the brass knob. This door was locked. She pressed the doorbell and waited.

Belinda realized no one was going to answer the door. She walked around to the garage and a side door opened. From the garage, she walked into the elegant home. Using her candle, she lit the flame and walked around the kitchen and into what looked like a den. The drawer was locked. She saw the rifles in the wood case. The case was locked.

She looked in the dining room and living room. She unlocked the front door. Next, she glanced in the family room. There appeared to be no one at home.

Walking up the stairs, she saw two little girls' rooms and a guest bedroom. Then she found the master bedroom. She put the candle on the coffee bar and jumped onto the comfortable queen-size bed. The mattress was plush and expensive. She took off her jacket, blouse top, and bra and threw them on top of the designer bedspread. Her skirt and underwear were next.

She opened the dresser drawers until she found the frilly underwear. Walking naked to the large closet, she held her candle. There were two expensive winter suits with the tags still on them.

Belinda saw the roller suitcase and put the open case on the bed. She started packing clothes into the suitcase.

"Six-hundred-dollar suits and three-hundred-dollar cashmere sweaters should work. The shoes don't fit."

There was a new box of shoes worth four hundred dollars in a box. There was a receipt inside. Belinda packed the shoe box.

She selected an expensive pantsuit to wear. Walking over to the low dresser, she picked up a perfume bottle and sprayed it. Belinda put the perfume in the case.

In the bathroom, she found some red lipstick.

"Ooh, red is a message. Kiss me, baby!"

On the outside of the mirror surface, she wrote a message. *Lost and Found.*

"He'll get the message."

Selecting a velvet designer red pantsuit to wear, Belinda walked out the front door with the suitcase. A rhinestone clip was in her hair and a shiny gold compact was in her pocket. Belinda was waiting for the last bus. No one paid her any attention. The woman appeared to belong in this neighborhood. By changing into more elegant clothes, she became invisible.

As the bus pulled away, the streetlights came back on. She looked at the large houses with lights in their living rooms. The people appeared happy.

Belinda knew happiness was an illusion. Money bought temporary joy. Taking the compact out, she looked in the tiny mirror. She looked different but knew she was the same. The fact that she was able to get inside Alec's house added to her cockiness. Her eyes changed in the mirror. There was hatred. She reminded herself to look again. This was who she was.

"The joy always rubbed off."

27 ALEC ARRIVED HOME

Alec was glad to be in Minneapolis. The time was about ten o'clock in the morning when he walked into his house. He dropped his stuff in his den and went upstairs to the master bathroom.

He rubbed his face. He needed a shave. Stepping into the coffee bar between the bathroom and master bedroom, he noticed his wife's dresser drawer wasn't closed.

He moved and gently closed the drawer. Going back to the coffee bar, he made himself a much-needed cup of coffee. There was some candle wax on top of the marble. He took a tissue and wiped the soft wax off.

"I don't remember my wife burning candles recently."

Alec used the facility and walked by the bathroom mirror. He reached the door jam and stopped.

He felt the hair raise on his neck. The room was wrong. Turning, Alec looked with horror at the red writing.

"Oh, no, we've had a break-in!"

He panicked and raced downstairs to get his revolver. Checking the rooms slowly with the gun in his hand, he made his way back upstairs to his bedroom.

He stopped and almost dropped the gun. He wanted to yell and hit the furniture. He looked at the long dresser mirror. The image was still there.

Alec saw the ugly, dirty clothes on his and his wife's bed and the open closet door. There were hangars on the floor in the closet. Someone stole his wife's clothes. He went to her jewelry chest. The diamonds and pearls were still there. He frowned. Most thieves stole expensive jewelry. Next, he looked in his nightstand. The white box was empty A yellow-amber butterfly necklace was missing.

It dawned on him who was in his home. He hated her even more. She violated his bedroom.

"I'm going to bring you down, Belinda."

He called the police and filed a report. Alec wanted every policeman in the state looking for the evil sick woman.

After the police left, he wiped the lipstick off the mirror and threw the ugly clothes in the garbage. He ripped the bedspread off. He rolled the spread into a ball and placed the cloth in a garbage bag. He took the bag to his car to take to the cleaners. The sheets were thrown in the washer and later the dryer. Normally he would have thrown the items away.

The price of the sheets was a thousand dollars. The bedspread alone was three thousand dollars. The spread matched the two thousand five-hundred-dollar drapes. His wife would be upset with him. That's why the items were cleaned.

He put the gun within reach on the bathroom counter. He shaved, took a shower, and dressed. Alec put the gun in his glove compartment and drove his expensive sports car to his office.

The receptionist told him about the odd woman who asked about his whereabouts. She described the woman. Alec told the receptionist about the power failure and break-in at his home. The building security was informed. They would be on the alert for any strange woman lingering in the halls. One of the security men remembered the odd woman with asthma.

Alec unlocked and stepped into his office. The yellow amber ball was in its place next to Amber's picture.

"At least she didn't desecrate my office."

Alec thought of a plan to catch her. Belinda wouldn't show near his home again, but she might show her face around his office. She would watch from the outside where she was more comfortable.

He called his boss and took a two-month sabbatical. He relocked his office and drove to the nearest thrift store.

Alec found the necessary clothes and disguise. He drove home, changed his clothes, and walked to the bus stop. The bus dropped him off at the coffee shop across from his office.

28 HOSTAGE ESCAPE

The bum squatted down on the sidewalk with his tin cup. He put a dollar bill and a few coins in the cup. Beat-up combat boots completed the poor look. The image was working as a man put in fifty cents. His boots were a little loose. While he sat, a small space was carved in the sole for a small thin knife. He sat there every day for two weeks.

Then he saw the woman that he was looking for. He recognized his wife's pantsuit and one of her new cashmere sweaters. Alec was glad his wife showed him the sweaters. This one was mint green.

The woman walked by his feet. Alec sniffed. He put his head down and yanked on his hat. The woman couldn't see his mad face. He mumbled. When she was half a block down the sidewalk, he watched her turn around. He kept his head down in a bowed position and pulled the faded handkerchief up over his neck. Alec swore under his breath. His haircut was too clean-cut.

"She stole not only my wife's clothes but her cologne. I'm going to strangle her slowly."

Belinda rubbed her neck as if someone grabbed her throat.

The next day, the bum sat in the same spot. He secretly watched the woman go inside the coffee shop and get a latte. He noted her hair was dyed auburn and cut straight. The tips of her hair barely touched her shoulders. She wore dark sunglasses.

"The black lipstick suits her."

Alec looked at her left hand. The hand was covered with a glove. The left-arm moved stiffly. He knew the woman was the elusive bad girl named Belinda Cummings.

Alec thought he should contact the police. The voice in his head warred with him. He couldn't trust anyone. She escaped from the others as easily as she breathed her crazy breath.

She came out of the coffee shop and walked across the street to his building. The bum didn't get up or follow the woman. There was no need. His office was secure. The woman didn't go inside but walked around the corner. He waited. She would reappear.

Alec was surprised Belinda was able to walk past the doorman. The man should have notified security. He realized the expensive clothes worked to her advantage. At the corner, she waited for the bus. He made his move when he saw the bus coming.

She entered the bus and so did Alec Rivers. The bum went to the back of the bus and slouched down low. He angled his hat, so she couldn't see his face. His face was dirtier than the day before and his beard was growing.

He saw her get off the bus. Alec waited until the bus turned the corner before he pulled the cord. The cord activated a bell. The bus went another block before stopping.

Alec ran through the backyards to see which house she entered. He stood behind someone's garage when he saw her come outside and talk to an old man watering the lawn.

He noted which house and walked down to the store he saw a few blocks from the house. Alec used the store's bathroom and bought a sandwich and water.

The sky darkened. He left the store bench and went down the street to the house. He saw the private entrance Belinda used.

Carefully trying the windows, he found one unlocked. Alec hid around the back of the garage and waited until two o'clock in the morning. He figured she should be asleep.

Slowly, he lifted the window and crawled inside. His eyes tried to adjust to the inside darkness. He stood up when something hit him in the head. Alec sunk to his knees and fell on his face. He was out cold. The iron frypan was thrown on the floor.

In the morning he awoke in a strange bed. His hands and feet were tied to the bedposts with rope. He touched the rope which was wet to tighten the knots.

Alec knew where he was. He was in Belinda's rental room. He needed to get the heck out of the area fast. His mind raced with what Belinda would do to him.

He moved his feet inside the boots. His leg bent until he could reach the heel. She missed his small knife hidden in the sole. She only found the larger one on the other leg. Using the knife to cut one leg rope, the other leg was also freed from the restraints. His one hand was loose, and he was working the other stubborn rope.

Alec was almost done with the last rope when he heard her voice coming through the wall. He finished with the rope and listened.

Belinda was talking with her rental manager about his gun collection. The man wouldn't budge on the price. The gun came with a silencer. Alec shot out of the open window and ran as fast as he could.

He ran two miles before he stopped. Luckily, she left his cell phone next to the bed. In his hasty retreat, Alec grabbed his phone. He stopped by a group of trees and called for a taxi. Climbing into the taxi, they drove to his office, and he changed his soiled clothes.

Quickly realizing his mistake, he called the police and gave them Belinda's rental house address. He decided that he was vulnerable. Alec Rivers needed massive help. When the police arrived at the rental, Belinda was gone. Her rental manager was dead, and one of his guns was missing along with the old man's car.

About a week later, they would find the rental manager's car in Lake City, Minnesota's boat harbor. The police believed she was using the Mississippi River and Lake Pepin as her gateway to freedom. There were many small river towns where she could disappear. Belinda could be anywhere.

Alec was beside himself for waiting too long to call the police. He wasn't thinking too clearly at the time. The image of the ropes around his hands and arms was too vivid. He itched from just thinking about her creepy sagging bed. Alec barely escaped.

He tried to get his wife to move back home. Gisele was thinking about their kids. They wanted to finish school where they were.

Alec thought Belinda wouldn't ever come back to Minneapolis or the surrounding area. He was wrong. Again, he underestimated her determination to obliterate those she hated.

29 REVENGE WAITS

A month passed, and Alec was working on a large legal case. His mind was preoccupied with building a defense for his rich client. The money mattered to him.

His usually neat office was filled with stacks of documentation and prior briefs. His team of young men used the large conference room to discuss the case.

Most nights Alec didn't go home but stayed in the spare room next to his office. He slept on the couch and ordered takeout.

Alec put the cardboard cartons down and stretched his legs. He called his wife and talked to his two girls. He missed his family and real life.

Looking out his office window, the weather showed rain. The rain began slowly and increased. Gray covered the sky, and the water ran into the drains. The people on the streets took cover except for one person.

The woman wore tall rubber boots, a raincoat, and carried a large umbrella. She was oblivious to the rain. She saw the man near the window. She knew who and what he was. There would be no mistakes the next time.

"Alec Rivers, your luck has run out."

On the weekends, Alec checked into a different hotel room. He showered and shaved. New shirts were purchased by his secretary. His office contained three suits and two new boxes of underwear. He didn't go home.

He dressed for Monday morning. This was their first court appearance. He wanted things to go well for his client. A few of his team accompanied him to the courthouse. They walked to the building. Entering the room where the judge would appear, Alec greeted his client and sat down. After three hours, his team walked back to the office.

They gathered in the conference room and ordered pizzas. Fresh pots of coffee were made, and chilly water was waiting on the counter. The team discussed their next move.

"We've been given two weeks to pull the rest of our evidence together. Let's get cracking."

Late that evening, Alec made a call to an old friend who owned a large cruiser.

"I need a respite. Would you mind if I take your boat out for a spin? I won't go far. I'm tired of staying in hotels. In three weeks, I get a break."

"Sure, Alec. I'll drop the boat keys and leave them with the receptionist.

"Thanks, man. I appreciate your friendship."

His secretary went to the department store and bought Alec casual slacks, a lightweight denim shirt, and a lined windbreaker jacket. She also bought him socks and tennis shoes. Alec thanked her. He told her he was too busy to shop for some casual clothes.

A woman watched Alec's movements. She didn't watch his secretary. The woman, however, noticed the secretary went shopping frequently and carried big bags.

"They must pay the secretary lots of money. I could do her job. I wonder where she lives. I bet she doesn't use the buses."

The tall building was too dangerous with all the cameras. The courthouse was even more so. The sidewalks were too crowded. The woman never knew which hotel Alec would stay. Hotels contained cameras and more security.

The woman thought about poisoning the food but couldn't figure out what to use, or how to get the poison in the meals. There also was a problem in that the wrong person could die.

She found a spot on the street to park her stolen vehicle. The car was repainted, and a different license plate was on the second stolen car. The woman had already ditched her rental manager's car.

It was Friday at noon when the opportunity presented itself. She saw Alec's team walk from the courthouse to his office. She waited to see if they would go into the large conference room on the second floor.

The team of lawyers didn't appear. The conference room was dark inside. She knew something was up. The woman raced to her car which was near his building's parking ramp exit.

Alec's sports car came to the end of the parking ramp. The woman climbed into her vehicle and started the engine. Her gas tank was full. She saw him pay the parking attendant. Alec turned the corner in front of her. She pulled out and followed.

Immediately both cars were on the freeway heading out of town. The woman kept a comfortable distance and turned south when Alec turned. She was familiar with the road.

He put his signal on to turn into a marina. The woman went down to the next exit and turned around.

She put her turn signal on and drove into the large marina. Her dad took her to this marina a long time ago. The place changed. There were sidewalks and large buildings. The docks were new, and the place could have been pictured in a magazine.

The woman saw Alec's sports car. She hoped that she wasn't too late. There were many boats in their slips. She looked at large powerboats and sailboats.

The hulls of the crafts gleamed when the sun hit their sides. The boat owners took diligent care of their expensive toys. The woman knew this place was exclusive. There was a nice restaurant a distance down the boat docks.

The woman changed her flats to black tennis shoes. She put her hair up and wore a black ball cap that matched her outfit. The sweatpants were new. She felt the gun holster under her top. The gun was loaded and ready. She undid the safety.

The woman walked by the restaurant and sat at one of the round cement tables with metal umbrellas outside. Alec was in the restaurant eating. She watched as the waitress poured more coffee. He dug out his wallet and paid cash for the meal leaving a large tip.

After an hour, she saw him walk toward a large cruiser called, *Raven Maven*.

The woman laughed for the first time in a long time. Then she stopped. It wouldn't do if she attracted his attention. Alec walked to the marina store to pay for gas. He didn't notice the woman.

She whispered to herself, "This might be my only opportunity to get aboard the cruiser."

The woman jumped at the chance to hide. She almost fell flat on her face by the power cord. She grabbed the boat's railing. The deck was slippery.

Belinda saw a rag in the boat's many cubby holes and dropped to the floor. She pulled herself backward and used the rag to clear her footprints. She heard whistling and disappeared below. She hid in a narrow closet. Her frame barely fit. She remembered her high school locker.

The good-looking lawyer came below and glanced around. He went topside and started the twin engines. The ropes were thrown from the dock onto the boat deck by a man across from the large cruiser.

"Enjoy your trip."

Alec thanked the man.

The woman in the closet felt the boat leave the dock area. She waited until the boat was in deeper water. She could feel the craft lift and go faster.

It was easy to step out of the closet.

30 A FUNERAL

Alec's wife, Gisele, stood with her two children near the casket of her husband. She couldn't believe he was gone. The strange woman must have hated him. The ceremony was over. Her parents led them to the waiting limousines hired for the event.

There was an after-funeral party at a hotel for the mourners. They went there and talked to people before going home.

The FBI and police would investigate Alec's death. After a week went by, she received a call.

Gisele answered a call from the department store regarding a box of shoes she returned. She was confused. Walking to her closet, she looked for the new box of shoes. They were gone.

She went back to the phone and talked to the store manager. The male sales clerk rang up the wrong price for the return. The store owed her fifty dollars more per the manager. Alec's wife asked the clerk to describe the woman. The clerk did. She wrote down the clerk's name and immediately contacted the police.

The police followed up, and the store showed the police the store video of the return transaction. The woman's face was visible. The person was not Mrs. Alec Rivers.

Alec's wife helped identify her husband's murderer.

Alec Rivers was killed with one bullet to his forehead. They figured he was steering the cruiser at the time of his death. He died instantly. The bullet was the same caliber as a gun owned by a man with a rental home in Minneapolis.

The cruiser was found in LaCrosse, Wisconsin, parked on an island. The anchor was secured in the sand. The dinghy was missing.

The boat was dusted for fingerprints. None were found. A woman's perfume bottle was left in the bathroom with some new underwear.

Alec's wife recognized her cologne and underwear. Gisele Rivers became upset. The next day she became mad. She would do everything in her power to help the police.

Gisele notified the media about Belinda Cummings and her horrible tactics to reach her husband. Mrs. Rivers begged people to turn the vicious killer into the police or any leads they found. The death of Alec Rivers became sensational news.

Rowell saw one of the news videos. He couldn't believe Belinda murdered Alec and an old man. Now he knew how dangerous Belinda was. He only guessed about Bev's death. Mrs. Abrams' death was out of character for Belinda. He knew Belinda's madness was increasing, and all concept of good was disintegrating.

Rowell went to his garage and turned the sander on. He worked two hours before he stopped. The sander was cleaned and put away. He covered the wooden coffin with a tarp.

"Come here, Belinda. I'll be waiting."

PEPIN

31 FALLOUT

Belinda watched the same news program as Rowell.

"I'm a victim of fallout. Returning those expensive shoes was a mistake. The sales clerk cheated me. What a dork! I should go kill him except I can't go to Minneapolis. The place is running with rats."

She knew the cologne and underwear were wrong to leave behind. Belinda left them to hurt Alec's wife. Her hatred and revenge overflowed the day when she killed him and escaped. The wife was getting her revenge by engaging the media on her side.

Belinda smiled.

The look on Alec's face was first stunned and then fear. He knew that his time on this earth was up. He took the cruiser's shift and pushed it forward, hoping to dislodge her from the doorway opening. She fired and then fell. The bullet barely made a noise.

Hastily, she had grabbed control of the throttle and slowed the boat before it ran aground. Her escapade killing Alec was a close one.

Belinda toured the water area and read the maps before she picked a spot to dump the cruiser. She was familiar with boats and engines. She had no problem lowering the dinghy, attaching the engine, and leaving the death scene.

164

She hitchhiked and saw an old rundown barn on the edge of Pepin. Belinda watched as the farmer fed his cows. The field smelled bad. After two days, she became bored.

"I need to get away from this shitty place. I could walk into town. Not during the day, because people will recognize me."

She took the rusted scissors and broken mirror and cut her hair off. Belinda looked like a man. The red hair was almost gone. The roots were black.

She stole an old jacket from the farmer. She saw him leave the jacket near the milking stall door.

There was a plan formulating in her brain.

"Rowell must have heard by now that I murdered Alec. He won't appreciate my arriving on his doorstep. He's the only person close by that lives alone and has money. He also has a truck. No one will expect to find me at his house."

She walked down to the Pepin pier and ate two rollups that she bought at the small gas station. The amount of meat was puny. The price was low, and the rollups quieted her noisy stomach. She opened her pop can and took a bite out of an apple.

All the pills from the flowerpot were gone. There was no way she could get more pills. Rowell was healthy as a horse. Her hand shook.

The boaters were washing and cleaning their crafts after a weekend of sailing. Belinda turned around and watched the boaters leave.

"A small sailboat might be easier to break the lock on the doorway. There might be drugs. The nursing home was to blame for her addiction."

She found an older sailboat. The outside paint job wasn't very professional. The young couple left the dock area. Belinda watched them drive away, and the apple core was tossed into the lake.

"I need some tools."

She emptied her pop can and crushed the soft aluminum. Throwing the can in the garbage, she walked to the gas station-hardware store. Buying a rubber hammer, screwdriver, and pliers, she paid for her purchases and left.

When she arrived at the small sailboat, she looked around. There was a small tarp on one of the boats. The woman grabbed the tarp.

Stepping on her selected craft, she hid under the tarp placed near the door latch. Belinda worked on the rusted metal until the screws were released. She could live on the boat until Friday morning. The young couple would be back, and she would be gone. She looked in the medicine cabinet and found a prescription. She popped two pills in her mouth.

Belinda could relax her guard and work on her methods to approach Rowell. The daring surprise worked in the past. However, she needed to be careful. He was strong and owned deer rifles.

She didn't know about the changes Rowell made to his yard. Belinda should have been suspicious. She also wasn't familiar with the new phones and forgot to see if he owned one. Recent technology escaped her and wasn't in her skill set.

Many things could be operated through an App on a cell phone. Rowell installed several important Apps on his phone. There were a few remotes throughout his home as backups.

32 ROWELL'S PRIOR IDEA

He peered through the scope of the gun and pulled the trigger. He cocked the barrel and did a repeat. The cartridges were not in the gun. The next time he pulled the trigger, there would be firepower.

"That's for innocent Bev Dawson. This pull on the trigger is for Amber Wood."

He wore gloves as he touched the gun. This gun was an older model. Rowell went to a spot on his wood floor. He moved the wool rug and put the gun in the spot. The wood fit back into the floor. The rug was placed on top.

No one knew about this gun. Rowell needed to hide this gun. One night, he messed up.

"It was an accident. How was I supposed to know the old man would decide to walk to his home? He frightened me."

Rowell ran his hand through his hair. His whole life was a screw-up except for football, the military stint, and finding work with the fracking company. The pay was exceptionally good. He made enough money to retire early.

The night in Minneapolis haunted him. He shouldn't have been there on Amber's street. Belinda haunted him even more.

"She's the one who scared Amber away by killing Bev. This is the only explanation for Amber's disappearance. For all I know, Belinda killed Amber. We just haven't found a body. Now the FBI is looking for Belinda. There is no doubt in my mind she used Mrs. Abrams and killed her. There may be many others besides Alec and an old man."

Rowell felt like contacting the writer lady. Somehow, he misplaced her business card.

"Way to go! I guess that I could ask the sheriff for her number."

Rowell paced the floor.

"Okay, bright boy, what are you going to tell the writer. You have no proof. She's smart. She might guess the crime that you committed. Your cushy life would be over."

He wanted to go to the bar and play pool. Rowell decided not to go. The locals would stare at him. They expected him to do something great. He was the star quarterback.

"Killing Belinda would make him a hero. Where did she go? The police won't say anything."

Every night Rowell watched the news and waited. He installed a new dish and service, so he could get the stations in Minneapolis. He knew Alec Rivers worked for a law firm in Minneapolis before he died.

"Alec was probably an excellent lawyer judging by the size of his house and office building. He shouldn't have gone on the boat. Belinda knows these waters."

Rowell watched as the lawnmower guy drove his equipment off the flatbed truck. He hired someone to do his lawn. Rowell couldn't stand the grass. The green stuff made him sneeze and he could afford one tiny luxury.

"I should hire the garden people in Stockholm to bulldoze all the grass and put it in river rock. I might save money eventually. No, I can buy my little tractor and do it myself. One three-foot square at a time."

He checked his savings account and grabbed his checkbook. He was going to the large handyman store in Red Wing. They carried small tractors with buckets.

Rowell was developing an idea in his brain.

Calculating how many tarps and river rock he would require, he did a schematic drawing of his yard, house, and garage. He put an X in one spot in the yard.

The spot was hidden by the house, the garage, the large LP tank, and some lavender bushes. He went outside and looked at the lavender bushes.

His neighbor would be able to see through the two bushes.

Rowell couldn't think of how to block the space. He went into the garage and saw an old wooden duck boat that was never used. The boat was four feet by six feet. If he flipped the boat on its side with some temporary posts, the boat would block the neighbor's busy eyes.

"I better get the rocks and tarp material delivered. A few six-by-six pieces of lumber might be required and some plywood. I could build a box. Oh, some treated timbers and posts are required to permanently prop the boat. A few roses in a garden in front of the boat would be nice."

Rowell was suddenly happy that he had something to do. His days would be busy. He stopped at a specialty garden store. The clerk showed him the roses they had in storage.

"The roses should be planted in about a month. We have some special fertilizers that you might want to purchase. Otherwise, they need pruning in the fall. Some foam covers are required for our harsh winters. Using two covers for each plant is recommended."

Rowell looked at the tags.

"You only have pink and red roses?"

"We'll get the white and yellow ones in about two weeks."

He was satisfied. "Can I order three yellow rose bushes now? You can call me when they arrive."

The clerk took Rowell to the cash register, and he paid for the fertilizer and the yellow roses. He loaded the bags on the seat of his truck. The bed was for some of the items from the handyman store.

He stopped at the rib place and ate lunch. He saw some people from Stockholm and nodded to them. Rowell sat in his booth and ate alone.

After getting some tools he decided he might need the treated timbers. He drove home. In the garage, he sawed the timbers the length required for the garden. Rowell pushed the built timbers on their sides until the prior night's dusting of snow disappeared.

"I better change the plan and make the plots six feet by six feet."

Rowell knew Belinda would steal his guns, truck, and money when she ran out. He was a sitting duck.

"The object is to not be a sitting duck. She gets to be the stupid one this time. Mistake number ninety-nine, Belinda, you're the freaking sitting duck."

33 CARA MANUS

Renee continued her search on the internet for a Cara Manus. She found a hit in Anacortes, Washington. There was a birth certificate for the child. She couldn't get a copy, but at least she knew a name.

The child's name was Catherine Ann Manus.

Cara never married that she could find out. Renee dug through her notes. Mrs. Wood mentioned a housekeeper who had an accident. The woman broke her leg on the Wood's steps and never appeared to heal. Mrs. Wood told her the name was Agnes Denton who currently lived in a nursing home.

The writer used the navigation map and found four nursing homes within twenty-five miles of Mrs. Wood's house. Calling each of them, she found the woman and made an appointment to visit her.

Flying to Minneapolis, Renee drove the rental car to the nursing home and parked the car. The weather was February, and the winds were super brisk. After her meeting, she planned on driving past the cabin and eat at the winery. She would stay overnight at the local hotel.

The orderly on duty ushered the woman into a visitor's room. The woman was nicely dressed and held a coverlet over her knees.

"Hello, Ms. Denton. I'm the writer, Renee Kendra from Arizona."

"Everybody calls me Agnes around here. You want to know about Connie and Cyrus?"

"Yes, more specifically Connie's sister, Cara. She was the one who died in a climbing accident, and there was a child."

Agnes developed a faraway look.

"Cara's boyfriend blamed himself and his sporting goods store. They fired him naturally. He thought his firm purchased a rope from a cheaper company that frayed. Her rope frayed apart on a rock. It was a sad day. I tried to convince Connie to take the little girl who was four years old at the time."

"Why didn't the Woods take the child?"

The old woman readjusted her coverlet. "Good question. Cyrus wanted to right away. Connie, however, wanted to have children of their own. The boyfriend worked odd jobs at the food-and-go gas station. After a year, he went to jail for robbing one of the stores he was responsible for. Bad move."

Renee walked over to the bottle machine and selected chilly water for herself and Agnes.

"Thank you. Cyrus flew to Seattle immediately. He found the little girl eating macaroni and cheese. Cara's boyfriend taught her how to use the microwave. Leaving a child alone is a no-no. The social workers were appalled. Cyrus had no problem bringing the child to Minneapolis."

Renee and Agnes drank their water.

"Cyrus made arrangements to bring Cara's body here, and she is buried in a local cemetery. He played with the child and hired two tutors and two nannies for her. Connie started to love the child when her doctor told her she wouldn't have children."

The orderly checked on Agnes who told the person to go away because she was busy.

"They purchased yellow-amber pieces for the child when she was first born, and they continued the presents each birthday."

"I know. Mrs. Wood showed me the collection," volunteered Renee.

"Was the little girl's name originally Catherine?"

Agnes laughed.

"There was much discussion in the house about what the Woods should call the child. The papers were waiting with the lawyer. They decided to call the child Amber. I was sworn to secrecy about the name. Now that Amber is missing, I don't think it matters if I tell you. I want your story to be correct. We need to find her."

"Thank you, Agnes. I appreciate our nice chat. Mrs. Wood has told me a lot of things about Amber, but she kept silent about the child."

Agnes wiped a tear. "I hope they find Amber. I would like to see her."

Now it was Renee's turn to sympathize. "Yes, we would."

"The Wood's pay my living arrangement here after the government pays. They have been good to me and my family."

"I didn't know this information," said Renee.

"Cyrus used to visit when he was alive. How is Connie doing?"

Renee hesitated.

"She seemed fine the last time that I talked to her."

The orderly again came into the room and Renee noted the time. Agnes leaned over.

"We better be quick with our conversation. Connie was particularly good at hiding her feelings. Even at the funeral for Cyrus, she didn't break down. I cried. She did come to visit me after the funeral. She told me Cyrus developed cancer and was dying. The person who killed him saved her husband from a lot of pain. She hugged me and said everything will be okay. How can things be okay?"

Renee left Agnes and told her she would send her the book when completed.

Renee drove past the cabin. She called her husband when she reached the winery.

"There are huge icicles here."

He laughed. The next morning, she drove by Mrs. Abrams' house and pulled to the far right on the road. The yellow police tape was gone, and there was an auction sign in the yard.

Renee took the bouquet she bought to place them on the porch. She saw a vase holding milkweed pods. There were two homemade color crayon drawings of birds with massive amounts of clear tape on the outside. Someone didn't want the rain or snow to destroy the gift cards.

Renee turned the bird pictures over. The boys signed their names, Henri, and Rob. There were large hearts around Mrs. Abrams' name. She placed her flowers next to their vase on the small table. Renee tucked her business card inside the stiff plastic. The little wooden bird was the only thing Renee had to remember the teacher.

"Rest easy, my friend."

There didn't seem to be much else she could do. Renee drove to Sheriff Edward's office and visited him. There was no news regarding Belinda's whereabouts.

She drove past Rowell's house. He didn't appear to be home. She stopped anyway and walked to the back door. After knocking she looked around.

A huge old boat was blocking the neighbors from seeing into his yard. She figured there was some type of dispute. Usually, people put up eight-foot fences.

Renee could see the rectangle of treated lumber. She figured he was putting in a small garden. She saw a nice wooden sign that looked carved. Taking her cell phone, she took a picture.

Making the image larger, Renee read the sign, *Amber's Flower Garden*. She was mildly surprised. She decided to not leave a note and drove back to the hotel. In the morning, she returned to Phoenix via a warm airplane.

"I should have left Rowell a note."

34 TRIXIE AND SHOCK

Renee watched a woman in her late thirties walk past the large fish tank at the mall restaurant in Scottsdale. The female was gorgeous, wore a tight-fitted coral-red dress, and matching high heels with gold studs. Her makeup and nails were impeccable. She recalled Rowell's comment about Trixie. His description of the cheerleader was perfect.

She stood up, and the woman came to her table. The woman threw her white coat over a chair. The designer bag was dropped into the other chair. With elegance only a model can maneuver, the woman sat down.

"Hi, I'm Trixie. My last name was Moran. I love to eat at this restaurant chain. Their fish is fresh, and their menu is one of the best. You picked an excellent choice."

After ordering sushi, they both started talking at once.

"You go first. Star and Mrs. Wood mentioned you," said Renee.

Trixie swallowed. This meeting was necessary.

"I met Amber Wood while at our second game. My group of cheerleaders didn't talk to the Pepin girls. We were enemies. Amber walked up to me and said hello. She told me my uniform was especially well designed and made me look great. Then she told me about a magazine that showed some new jumps our group might want to try. She gave me her magazine."

Renee could see Amber being friendly to everyone she met. There was no one she talked with that said anything negative about her.

"Amber traveled with her family extensively and met lots of different nationalities. She knew French, Chinese, and a few other languages. Plus, she watched how her parents treated others with respect. Amber was the same."

Trixie fluffed her mid-length hair.

"I was blown away by her. We started talking about girl stuff and finally, we halted our conversation because the game started. We talked again at halftime and agreed to meet for lunch in the future. We saw each other once a month while she lived in Pepin."

"Mrs. Wood did tell me that you both were remarkably close. I gave her a call after talking with Star. Mrs. Wood sent me your picture."

Trixie knew which picture Amber took with her tiny camera.

"We became close. Amber and I made a pact that after she went to Minneapolis, she would let me know if everything was okay by sending me a book of poems with a four-leaf clover. Girls back then made a lot of pacts. I wasn't sure she would follow through. I hoped she would."

Renee found the pact interesting until Trixie handed her a small box with the postage stamp on the outside. The date was six months after Amber's disappearance.

Renee opened the box. Inside was a small book of poems. She opened to the satin marker. Inside on the page wrapped in plastic wrap was a compressed four-leaf clover.

"Oh, my gosh! This means Amber didn't disappear. Or is this a fake joke? Someone else knew about your pact?"

Trixie smiled.

"No one knew. I met Amber's father once. He was very cordial. I could tell he loved Amber and her mother right away. He doted on his daughter. I believe the father helped Amber disappear."

Renee paged through the book to the last poem. In yellow highlight, three words were circled, *do not tell*. There was a large handwritten initial "A".

"Explain why you are telling me about this pact and showing me this book. Does Mrs. Wood know about the pact?"

Trixie watched as the waitress left their food. She picked up a crab roll and ate a bite.

"Mrs. Wood contacted me. Your card and your visit mattered. She liked your spunk. In other words, you were authentic in her book, which is huge. She asked that I show you, so you might understand."

Renee's eyes grew wide. She finally felt included by the Wood family. The realization made her feel good inside.

"Of course, Mrs. Wood has known all along that her daughter wasn't missing. That is why she was so calm when I visited her. They have hidden their daughter all this time for her safety. The reason for the secrecy is they believe someone still wants to harm her."

Trixie agreed that there could be a killer waiting if the truth were known. Renee shook her head in shock.

"Why tell me the information? I'm not completely understanding. This part can't be put in the book."

Trixie finished her lunch, and Renee tried to eat a few pieces.

"Amber was in Minneapolis visiting her mom recently. She decided to go shopping downtown. Her rental car was still in the parking ramp. Mrs. Wood called the rental agency to pick up their vehicle. Amber never came back home. She knows how to get a taxi or take a bus or fly to another continent. Amber did have her purse and passport with her. However, she is now really missing."

Renee tried to digest the horrible information.

"Mrs. Wood has hired a private investigator. His name is Kelly Masters. If there is any way you can help us find her, we would appreciate it."

"Has Mrs. Wood gone to the police?"

Trixie frowned.

"Mrs. Wood can't ask the police. She doesn't trust their workforce and the knowledge could create more problems."

Renee got the picture. "You are right. There would be a lengthy investigation, and Mrs. Wood could be charged for obstruction. Finding the real Amber would get lost in the maize of confusion."

"We're hoping that Amber might have figured out something important to her case, and she fled the area. Maybe she saw someone with something they shouldn't have. Or she saw someone from her past that scared her. We don't know. Right now, we're in a holding pattern."

The waitress brought the check, and Renee gladly paid for their lunch. Alec Rivers once had a small office in downtown Minneapolis until he joined a large firm.

"Would she have checked up on one of her old boyfriends while she was there or chatted with his wife?"

Trixie's eyes darkened, "I hope not. I think Amber is smarter than that. He was in her past permanently."

Renee wondered how in the world she was going to finish her book. Things were developing into a strange arena of characters.

"As you said, Amber is pretty smart. If she is in danger, she will go underground. Mrs. Wood might want to rethink the investigator."

Trixie thought about her comments.

"I'll let her know."

"Good, I believe Amber will give her mother a signal. She might also send you one. If she does, promise me that you will let me know."

Trixie sighed, "I will. I suppose if she reappears, you will want to meet with her?"

Renee grabbed her bag and coat, and Trixie did the same.

"I most definitely want to meet Amber. I think that between the two of us, we might be able to put the pieces of this puzzle together. I have some theories that scare me if they are true. One of those theories is that someone is lying."

Trixie watched some teenagers walk by them. They were laughing and having fun. She and Amber used to be young.

"And we both know lying is toxic."

Renee knew there was one more question.

"Do you know if Amber was adopted by Mr. and Mrs. Wood?"

Trixie looked surprised.

"I never thought to ask. The idea is not impossible. I'm not sure. Would an adoption make a difference?"

"That's okay. I'll carefully ask Mrs. Wood for confirmation."

Trixie hugged Renee and promised to stay in touch. They both wanted whoever was out there caught and locked away.

Renee found her car in the mall parking lot. She was relieved Amber didn't fall under evil people twenty years ago. She was glad she made a life for herself.

Amber was now a medical teacher at a university in Vancouver, Canada. Currently, Amber was on a three-week break. Renee hoped Amber would turn up real soon.

"Or rather, I should say that I hope Dr. Catherine Ann Manus shows up soon. She could bow out of her teaching duties for the next term or stop altogether."

She started the car and knew she would need to keep part of her conversation with Trixie and her newly found knowledge a secret from her husband. The fewer people that knew about the recent events and name change, the better.

Renee knew Agnes wouldn't tell. No one knew about her conversation with Agnes. She thought about contacting Mrs. Wood.

"Catherine might have seen Belinda accidentally is my guess. Or Alec's death scared her."

When Renee arrived home, her husband was waiting.

"How did things go? Any added information?"

She put her purse and briefcase down.

"Lots of good stuff from Agnes from my trip to the Midwest. She was a genuinely nice lady. Today with Trixie helped immensely. Trixie was a sweetheart. You would have liked her looks and spirit. I forgot to mention that when I was in Pepin, I talked to the local sheriff, drove by Mrs. Abrams, and stopped at Amber's first boyfriend's house. Rowell wasn't home."

Her husband hugged her. "Well, at least you are home safe. There's no need to travel until spring. I bought some hamburgers for supper with potato salad. There's a broccoli salad for me. Also, we have slices of carrot cake."

She was glad her husband was thinking about fun stuff like food.

"I'm thinking we should take the RV to Vancouver sometime. But that means that I would need to get a passport and so would you."

"Sure, we can think about it next month. I really would rather go to the cabin and get the garden in early this time."

Renee sighed and kicked off her shoes. The dog kept following her. He wanted a pet and for her to sit down. She finally collapsed in a chair. The dog jumped up next to her and squeaked his toy. She threw the dog toy as far as she could in the living room. Her husband brought her a drink.

"Tired?"

"I am fried."

They went to bed early. Thoughts of the Amber person or Catherine were gone from her tired brain. She needed two months off.

The next day she did check how many air miles a round trip would take to Vancouver and back from Phoenix.

"Ouch. I'll wait until I can visit with Mrs. Wood."

She finished a few more chapters of the book. She knew her husband could read the writings. A second copy was on a shared drive on their computers. He never did read the chapters until she was all done. The reason he didn't read the book was that she always changed the draft one more time.

"Mrs. Wood likes perfection. I do, too," commented Renee.

She received the call the next day from Sheriff Edwards. He told her there were a few drops of blood in the doorway of the cruiser. The blood wasn't Alec's. The blood type match was the same as Jane Doe. Jane was Belinda Cummings, and the conclusion was made that she did, in fact, coldly track and kill Alec Rivers. There was an arrest warrant out for the person.

Renee informed her husband.

"This story is getting too dangerous. Maybe you should lay low."

"Yes. I see things heating up. However, I need to talk with Alec's wife. There is more that must have happened before his death. I must understand the movements Belinda made before she killed Alec."

"Okay," surrendered her husband.

The story was taking shape in her mind. Events were falling into tidy categories. She was glad Amber was alive. That category was the standalone, biggest of events currently.

"I believe Belinda taunted Alec and his family before she killed him. She liked to manipulate the scene to her liking. I believe she tracked Alec's movements. She has a pattern or plans most of the time. However, she rapidly adapts to a different scene."

Her husband replied, "I see one scary control freak."

"Exactly my impression of a full-blown crazy personality."

35 BINOCULARS

Rowell sat in his truck close to a hamburger joint at the end of the Pepin pier. He rolled his truck window down. He opened the paper wrapping and checked the patty bun to make sure the girl added extra pickles. The pickles helped.

"No need for ketchup."

The bun was toasted. He put the hamburger together and took a large bite. He took his binoculars from their hard case.

Slowly he scanned the boats on each dock one by one. The boats were mostly devoid of their owners. There were a few people who lived on their boats. Rowell knew all those live-aboard people.

He stopped chewing. Rowell put the half-wrapped hamburger on his lap. He looked again and watched someone with short hair on a small sailboat. The person turned, and he could tell this was a woman. He zeroed in on the face.

Rowell lowered his binoculars.

"Gotcha!"

He picked up his half-eaten hamburger and threw it on the dashboard. Rowell started the truck and drove away. There was no need to contact the sheriff. None of the police organizations knew where the woman went. Her ability to run and hide was phenomenal. They didn't think the way she did. Rowell knew her extremely well. He remembered third grade vividly.

"She is staying on the boat while the owners are away. If they arrive this weekend, she will either move to a different boat or find a new place."

He stopped by the store and purchased some nice ribeye steaks, lettuce, tomatoes, dressing, and homemade bread. The store knew a woman who brought in the bread each week. The townspeople hit the store in the early morning to get a loaf.

The clerk asked, "Why, Rowell, are you having company this weekend? Should I spread the word that you have a date?"

"Penny, you know that I only have eyes for you. It's not my fault your husband keeps you on a short leash."

"Nice distraction. Have fun!"

Rowell grinned wickedly. "I do make my fun."

"We like your new yard. I'm glad you bought the rusty ornaments from the guy in town. He needs the money."

Rowell appreciated a guy who welded things together. He avoided the painted ones.

"The ornamentation does look nice. They keep your eyes busy with their movement. Just last week my friend drove over the curb trying to watch one of the spinners."

"Your friend wouldn't be the one living in an apartment across the pier?"

Rowell nodded and left the store. He purchased some gas in a can at his favorite station. He went inside to pay. The owner knew there was no more grass in his yard.

"Why do you need gasoline?"

Rowell thought for a minute.

"I'm thinking about getting a small fishing boat. I'll try the aluminum ones or something with a huge bottom."

"Good choice. Your duck boat is landlocked."

Rowell slapped his friend on the back.

"See you around, old man."

"Hey, I'm not old. I'm only a year older than you."

"My point exactly."

Rowell waved to his friend and took the gas can home. He poured the gas into a special device he built. He placed the control piece on top. There wasn't time to test this device.

There were other devices along the garage wall. His backyard was one big boobytrap. The front yard was safe. He installed a cement mermaid fountain that filled with water in the summer.

The dogs liked to drink from the low fountain as did the birds. Rowell wondered who would take care of his house when they put him in prison.

"Oh, well, a person can't have fame and pleasure. One thing or other needs to drop."

He walked to his backyard and peeked at the rose bushes he planted. The frost hadn't touched them. Rowell could hardly wait until summer when the yellow flowers bloomed.

He touched the sign that he made. Rowell knew everything was ready. He also knew Belinda would use a gun.

"She'll use one of her stolen guns for sure."

He already checked on the internet all the types of straps and devices a person could use to conceal their weapon. Rowell used his computer to decorate a body image with the devices. He saved the images and reviewed them daily.

There was a fish fry every Friday at the local winery. He sighed. This Friday would not be a suitable time to eat fish. He dug in his clothes to find some tattered-looking jeans and a grayed T-shirt. He found an old green windbreaker and brown hat.

Rowell would be in an apartment near the water. The view of the boat docks would be visible. He rented the room for a week from his friend. His friend was flying to Miami to visit a sister.

He packed himself two large sandwiches, a bag of chips, bananas, pop, and chocolate twinkies. At the last minute, he threw in a gun with two clips and his binoculars. His cell phone was in his pocket.

Rowell went to the second-floor apartment and watched the small sailboat. He saw Belinda leave and sit on a bench on the pier. She stared at the waves endlessly.

The young couple didn't arrive at the pier by eleven in the evening. Rowell was about to pack his binoculars away when he saw the couple arrive. This time they brought a mongrel dog.

"Well, I'll be a monkey's uncle. They went to the pound and bought the dog. There won't be anyone getting near their boat now."

Rowell moved the binoculars to the pier bench. The bench was empty.

"Darn it. She disappeared on me."

Rowell scanned the pier and saw a head disappear down by the beach. He knew she was going to travel the beach and walk up some steps further down. There were houses close to the railroad steps. He knew she would try to find an empty house.

Rowell was at a loss. He wasn't sure if he should follow her or not. He knew his house was secure. There were signs from the security company that he hired.

Rowell decided to try to get some sleep. She might try to find another boat after the weekend was over. He would wait.

36 BOAT ARRIVAL

He sat up in his friend's apartment bed. Rowell's body was in a sweat. He was back in a strange country battling the enemy. His unit was broken off from the others. Their bullets were low.

He took his military knife out and started checking the ground for a piece of wood so that he could make darts. The darts would need to be strong and sharp.

Rowell shook his head from the flashback. This was not a fun time to remember his past. The bedroom was in the back, and the shades were slightly up. He picked up two darts from the bedside table and threw them one by one at the dartboard.

"Perfect hit."

The darts slowly fell off the board onto the floor. He examined the cork. The cork was crumbly.

Rowell ran his hands through his hair and looked at the time on his cell phone. The time was five o'clock in the morning. He went to the bathroom and back to the chair where his binoculars lay.

He saw her sitting on the pier bench again. He was wary of her following a certain pattern. She lived in this area for eighteen years. She never liked the river before. Rowell slid down to the floor and stared at the ceiling. Wishing her gone from his town didn't work.

Rowell kept asking himself if he could kill Belinda. He didn't want to kill her, but she would give him no choice.

"She was always bad. Her behavior has worsened over time. No jail will hold her. I can't let her get at Amber if she's even alive."

He checked his voicemail messages. The boat, trailer, and motor he ordered arrived in Red Wing. Rowell could pick up his boat. He was excited. The final piece of his equipment would be here.

"Let's dump this cat and mouse game for now."

Rowell went down the backstairs and hiked to another friend's house where he left his truck.

He picked up his boat with a new canvas top and drove home. Backing the boat in his driveway, he unhitched his truck.

Not much time passed before the sheriff drove by and made a U-turn. The sheriff parked his car on the curb and stood next to Rowell.

"The new boat is an absolute beauty. Take the cover off. I want to see inside."

Rowell did as he was told. Sheriff Edwards climbed inside.

"See, I told you that I was going to purchase a boat. You didn't believe me. I want to see you smiling when I go flying by in my boat and wave."

The sheriff couldn't help but smile. "I can picture you waving your silly hat going twenty miles an hour max. When are you going to try her out?"

Rowell shook his head. "I probably should read the manual, so I don't blow up the engine."

"Nah, I never read the manuals, and I'm still alive."

Rowell looked at the sheriff in disbelief.

"How big a fish would you think I can catch?"

Sheriff Edwards scratched his head.

"There is this one spot in the river that's about fifty to sixty feet deep. Some of the fishermen have told stories about large fish in the spot. Most of us think there is a lot of baloney in those stories. Yet, there have been big bones on the shore."

"I bought the depth finder and fishing contraption. Where exactly is this place?"

The sheriff pointed at the spot on the map that Rowell pulled from his truck.

"There are many spots. Look at this map. I didn't realize the depth rings until I bought my boat."

The sheriff climbed out, and Rowell placed the cover over and secured the lines.

"I might take her out some evening and turn the lights on. Usually, the lake is quiet at night. You can hear the fish jumping," commented Rowell.

The sheriff nodded.

"You might want to get some nets at the hardware store. Those old nets of your dads are rotten. You might need a new fishing line. A good rod and reel always will help."

Having dispensed with good information, the sheriff walked over to his vehicle, started the car, and went to the local hotel for lunch. He would relay the news about Rowell's boat.

Rowell drove to Wabasha and bought new fishing gear. When he came back, he knew someone opened his back gate and his back door. He opened his garage. The security box wasn't lit.

He put the fishing gear in the garage and closed the door. He locked his truck and put the keys in his pocket with his cell phone.

Rowell knew who was inside his house. She came sooner than he expected. She was a known killer. He studied killers. Each killer developed their signature or pattern. The pattern was important. If you missed the pattern, you were lost.

He knew her skills and techniques. She liked to play with her potential victims. Rowell knew he was her next target. He had no intention of being a victim. He was skilled beyond the normal person. Years of training automatically kicked in. He entered the game called war. Only one person would survive.

Instead of going inside, he went to his barbeque grill. He took off the cover, opened the lid, and turned on the gas. Once he was satisfied the bars were heated enough, he started scraping the old food from the grill grates. He put the grate brush on the hangar.

Rowell turned and went inside his house. He was calm. Every step was calculated and measured. Taking off his jacket, he took the steaks out of the refrigerator and unwrapped the white butcher's wrap. The paper was thrown in the garbage. The lid on the plastic garbage can did the usual swing back and forth.

Salt and pepper were applied to the juicy steaks. He washed his hands and found a large clear bowl. The lettuce was washed and drained. He washed and sliced the tomatoes into pieces. Rowell began tearing the lettuce into small wedges. He put the tomatoes on top along with some shredded cheese. The bottles of dressing were placed next to the salad.

Finding the foil in the cupboard, he ripped off a long piece. Taking a sharp knife, he found the butter and stopped.

Belinda was standing in his small living room watching him. He saw the large gun pointed in his direction. The gun didn't scare him. He lived around guns his entire life. Her appearance didn't unnerve him. He saw her before.

Rowell cut the bread into one-inch pieces and buttered the bread. He ignored her. Stepping over to the cupboard he turned the carousel until he found the garlic powder. Rowell sprinkled the garlic on the bread and wrapped the loaf in the foil.

He put all the items on the large tray and grabbed his tongs.

Belinda watched him. He wasn't afraid. Rowell was never afraid of her. She didn't know why.

"You should be scared out of your wits."

Rowell looked at her. The short hairdo was a terrible idea. He wasn't going to mention those thoughts. She might shoot him immediately.

"The grill is ready. Do you want to eat and talk first? You're still the same person from third grade. I warned you then. Belinda, what part of the words, *I know you*, don't you understand? No, I've never been afraid of you nor will I. The gun doesn't change my feelings. I've killed, and you've killed. Big deal."

Belinda motioned for him to go outside.

37 DARTS

Flipping the ribeye steaks, he told her they had four minutes before the meat was done. The smell of meat cooking made her want to eat decent food. Rowell was a superb cook.

"Why did you come back to Pepin? People are looking for you. Most of the town knows your face. Even with the short hair, they would know."

She touched her hair. "No one has recognized me."

He smiled. "You are wrong. I saw you on the small sailboat."

"You are lying."

He looked at her and shook his head.

"Again, same old Belinda. She doesn't believe me. The world is out to get only you. Am I correct in my assessment?"

He washed the large plate with a hose and took the steaks off. "No answer, I think we should eat inside. I'll get us plates, napkins, and silverware."

She followed him into the house. He collected the items and put them in a basket with cans of pop. He motioned toward the table.

Belinda looked at the kitchen and could see into the living room. The walls were devoid of pictures; no knickknacks existed on the small tables. There were no personal or family pictures. The house was sterile like poor people's homes or a military barrack.

"We eat outside. Your house is giving me the creeps. It's as if your parents are home watching us. Why didn't you move? This house is tiny. I hate tiny. Bev's sister, Bella, went weird whenever she was in a small space. She wore those tank tops with sayings."

Rowell found a large tray.

"This house was already paid for. Living here costs me little money even though the space is tiny. It's more room than I had in the desert. I didn't know Bev had a sister. You're making her up."

"Please, stop the pity party. You served our country and lived in the desert. Who cares? I don't. Bella was real. She was crazier than me."

Rowell slammed the tray down on the counter.

"Ooh, big sore spot. Not to worry, I won't talk about your military service. However, I saw a new boat. The expensive brand with a motor. The trolling motor is nice. The small motor works better than a seining net. You must have money to burn."

He sighed. She was trying to get to him. He almost fell for her sarcasm.

"There's one thing that bothers me. How did your arm get buried in the sand at the Deer Island beach?"

There was no reaction.

"Ah, you were with a young man when an accident happened. I'm sure he drove you to the hospital. Gangrene set in. Am I right?"

Her face was turning red.

"Still, the hospital does dispose of limbs. How did you get the limb?"

She looked at him as if she were going to kill him any minute."

"Let me guess. Maybe you stole the limb or had one of your followers do the snatch which would be an amazing feat. Guess hospital security was lax."

"I hate you. You called me a thief."

Rowell calmed his mind. Belinda was right where he wanted her. Frazzled and disoriented was the best way to end this story.

"I didn't call you a thief. I said maybe. But no one is crazier than you. Let's eat unless you are too mad."

Belinda picked up her knife and waved the sharp object in the air.

"At least, I don't use fire like my friend."

He grabbed the steak sauce.

"I guessed that Bella helped steal your arm. Burying it on Deer Island was a novel approach. Someday the arm would surface and create a stir. I remember some complaints about a disappearing car from one of the moms. However, I do recall a girl in town wearing tank tops. One comes to mind. So, it was the Bella girl who always *lit something*."

Rowell distributed the plates and utensils and pushed over the tray of food. He let her put the salad, bread, and cooked steak on her plate. She squeezed the salad dressing from the bottle and picked at the lettuce.

"You made Caesar salad without anchovies."

"The cupboard was bare. I'll get anchovies and the correct ingredients next time."

Belinda's eyes squinted. "There probably won't be an opportunity for a next time."

He did the same to his salad, grabbing the necessary items from the table. Rowell knew the steaks were cooked to perfection.

"Perfectly pink is the best. Not too raw and not too done."

She continued eating.

"Don't you just love a home-cooked meal?"

She looked at him drily. He handed her the steak sauce. She put the bottle down with a large thud. Rowell ignored the gesture.

Both ate their food in silence. Two-thirds of the way through the meal, he spoke again.

"You didn't comment about my new yard. I worked for a long time to get the outdoor décor to match my magnetic personality. The river rock is especially nice. I opted for rock rather than beach sand. Sand clogs the drain."

Her head jerked. "What drain? You are still full of shit, Rowell. The river rock is ugly. The stuff is free on the beach. Your cement fountain is horrible. Rusted metal is the worst design concept ever. The metal screams farmer. I saw a wooden sign. You were a jerk to like Amber and date her."

Her attack on his things was fine. Her attack on Amber wasn't. He told himself to remain calm.

"Now you have gone and spoiled my fun. Every dog in the neighborhood likes my fountain and has peed on the same spot. There's your reason for why the cement has turned green. Pee is considered an outside element. Then there are the squirrels. One more element. Don't talk to me about Amber. You never understood talented and nice."

Belinda stopped eating.

"You are so gross. Amber wasn't nice."

Rowell ignored her comments. He distracted her long enough.

"Do you remember when we used to play darts in the bar?"

"I do. You cheated."

Rowell smiled. "I did cheat. My friend, however, beats me every time. I'm going to invent a board and darts that make the playing field equal."

He cut another piece of his steak.

"You might not live long enough."

Belinda used her right arm for everything. He stood up. Her comment didn't sit well with him. This was the second reference to his demise. He knew she was getting ready to kill him.

She dropped her fork and picked up the gun. The steak knife was swiftly in the other hand.

"Don't move, Rowell."

He pushed the envelope as far as he could. There was one more move to make. The move would be expected because he was a jock. Rowell was good at deception on the field. She didn't know his mind was set to win. He stood up in defiance.

"I forgot to turn the gas off."

"Leave it and sit down."

Rowell sat down and ate a bite of garlic bread. She watched him.

"Aren't you going to ask me questions?"

"Nope, I read the newspapers, watch television, and have a fantastic brain."

Belinda's face contorted into a partial smile.

"You remember when I told you that I was more intelligent, more good-looking, and better at everything?"

"We're talking about third grade again?" asked Belinda.

"You do remember. Good."

"I disliked you then, disliked you in high school, and dislike you now."

"No, you didn't. Well, not at first anyway. I can understand today. Sometimes I don't even like myself," offered Rowell.

"Why don't you kill yourself?"

He looked at her eyes. The craziness was overtaking her. She was changing. He needed to act fast.

Belinda put the steak knife down and ate a bite of the garlic bread. "How do you know how to make this taste just right?"

He looked at the rose bushes. There were some buds on the plants. He could see yellow. He almost said yellow amber.

"Practice. The garlic bread takes a little more effort and time. My dad showed me. Breadmaking and how to make the dough rise was his forte. I usually buy the bread in town. But he taught me a lot of cool stuff plus the military."

"Your dad didn't play darts."

Rowell laughed, "My mom wouldn't let him. He wasn't particularly good."

Belinda didn't know what to do. She put the garlic bread down and looked at the gun. He noted she took the safety off at some point. He missed the flip on the button which was not like him.

Rowell stood up. She stood up.

"Look, you can shoot me if you want. I'm turning off the gas. Otherwise, you might blow both of us to kingdom come. Your aim might hit the barbeque when I run in that direction."

"Walk slowly and turn off the gas."

"Yes, ma'am."

Belinda waived the gun. "Don't call me names. I might blow both of us."

He raised his hands in surrender.

She watched as he went to the grill. Rowell noted that she was standing in the perfect spot. Her back was to the garage wall. He hoped her gun wouldn't fire. He thought to himself. "If I die, I'll know she has died, too."

Belinda didn't see him remove the phone from his pocket and touch the App button. He glanced briefly under the grill for the gas knob. Rowell touched the phone again. Then he turned off the gas and shut the grill lid.

There was no sound. She didn't discharge the gun. He was thankful. Rowell fumbled for the nearest lawn chair and sat down. He sat for half an hour. He didn't look toward the picnic table. He heard someone knocking on his front door.

Not completely focusing, he clumsily went to his front door.

"Mrs. Potter, how nice to see you."

Her dog was whimpering. Rowell looked down.

"Oh, no, your dog has tangled around the mermaid fountain again. I'll get her untangled."

He helped Mrs. Potter off his step and untangled the dog. He saw the dog mess.

"Oh, dear, she must have had an accident."

"Don't worry about the mess. I'll throw the job in the garbage and drag out the hose. The spot will be good as new."

Mrs. Potter sweet-talked to her dog. He waited.

"Thank you, Rowell. We like your new boat. Our woman's group voted, and we think you should go fishing soon. You catch a great big one and take a picture. You can send me the photo to my phone number. I'll have something to brag about at our next meeting."

"Sure thing, Mrs. Potter. Your number is in my phone under favorite people."

"We like you, too."

He closed the front door and walked through the house. There was no need to hurry. The darts did their job. The mechanism inside his garage released with abrupt precision when he pushed the second button. He was glad she sat on the correct side of the picnic table. His device worked.

Rowell thought about Mrs. Potter's comments.

"They like me and my new boat."

He reached the body. He pushed another button and the darts disappeared into the garage siding. He would need to disassemble the device later.

A beige painter's tarp was used to tidy up the form. Rowell pulled the wrapped form into his garage. The heavier dark green tarp on a table was thrown aside. The long-formed body was put into the plywood coffin. He nailed the lid all around. Next, he went outside and sprayed the cement, garage wall, and grass with the hose.

The paper plates and food were thrown in the garbage along with the food and silverware. He didn't need much silverware.

Next, he picked up the doggie doo and sprayed water around the front fountain.

"All is quiet on the front."

When it was dark, he unscrewed his outside garage light temporarily. The small tractor was used to hoist the coffin onto the boat. The boat cover sat nicely over the wood. There was no bulge. His measurements for the coffin were exact.

He screwed the bulb tight. The garage light turned back on.

Rowell packed a metal cooler with ice, frozen sandwiches, and breakfast burritos. He made a thermos of hot coffee and filled a jug with water. The fishing equipment was stored inside his truck.

At midnight, he drove down to the Deer Island cement ramp. The boat ramp in town was too well-lit. Releasing the boat, he parked the boat on the shore. The truck and trailer were pulled into a parking space.

Adele Strong opened her trailer door and saw the man. He waved. "New boat. I must try her out. Sorry for the noise. Fish like the night."

"No problem. My husband told me the fish were biting today. Let's hope they are still hungry," said Adele.

Rowell pushed the heavily-loaded boat into the water. The new engine started immediately. He turned on the boat's lights and watched his gauges. The boat was turned toward one of the deeper spots in the lake.

He slowed the motor when he saw a depth of fifty-two feet. Rowell drove back and forth over the spot.

"I shouldn't have fed her. She's heavier than the pine."

Finally, he pushed and lifted the wood over the side. The coffin splashed into the water. A strong rope was attached to a release mechanism to slowly lower the box.

Rowell hit the release. The coffin sunk immediately. He sat in the boat watching the rope. There were a few bubbles. The boat drifted while Rowell stared at the night. Finally, the rope line ended. He wound the line back into the mechanism.

The boat drifted a little more.

Rowell believed killing someone was never an easy thing. Before he started the motor and put her in a low idle. He thought he should say some words. His mind was stuck. Recall from church wasn't happening.

"Game over."

He revved the engine and drove away as fast as he could. With much relief, he did find the right words which were for himself and all her victims.

"There is justice in this world. May those victims rest in eternal peace."

A few stars came out and the display was poetically beautiful over the lake. He stopped the engine and felt grateful that Belinda hadn't won. The boat launch was close. He took an oar and checked the depth.

Rowell stepped out of the boat and waded to shore pulling on the front rope line. He tried to be quiet.

38 GARAGE EXTENSION

A year went by and there was no further sighting of Belinda. The town relaxed and people resumed their daily activities. The sheriff pulled next to the curb and walked into Rowell's backyard.

Rowell was surprised to see him.

"Your neighbors called me at six in the morning. Who gets up that early? Nobody. They said you were hammering loudly. I told them hammers do make a noise when an object is hit. I bet your neighbors don't own any tools. I told them I would check out their sorry complaint."

Rowell held up his hammer.

"Guilty. There's no room in the garage for my workshop since I bought the boat. I've laid out some wood planks and stakes to see if my space will be large enough."

"Permits?"

"No, I'm still trying to do the figuring and cost."

The sheriff walked around the space. The grass hadn't yet been removed there. The weeds were thick. It was the only spot in the yard with grass. "I thought the landscapers took out the grass."

Rowell knew he should have parked some gravel in the backyard. Sheriff Edwards scratched his head.

"It's hard to tell. You should have mowed the weeds first. No, you can't mow the weeds. Too much noise."

Rowell disgustedly looked at the weeds.

"No lawnmower and therefore, no noise. You are safe from another call. I'll probably need some gravel fill."

"Yep. I'd go bigger. Men like a nice workshop. You could buy a loud saw or a huge vacuum. Ten thousand Rpms would fit the bill. No, make that one hundred thousand. I wouldn't mind another call."

Rowell wasn't listening. He wasn't sure the investment would ever come back to him if he sold the home. The sheriff saw his hesitation.

"What's the real issue, son?"

Rowell motioned the sheriff toward the house. Inside, he poured them both a glass of lemonade. "I might move to Seattle or Canada."

"Oh, oh, there's a female in this story. I can see stars happening in your future."

Rowell let his breath out. "I don't know. I love her but she can't seem to see me. I see her. Plus, I'm not exactly a nice person."

The sheriff waved his hands. He wondered if Rowell found a new girlfriend.

"Women are tough. I did have another reason for my visit. There is an investigator that wants to talk with you. We heard about a sighting of Belinda here a year ago. There was a recent one near the pier. It would have been natural for her to contact an old high school friend."

"I was never Belinda's friend, and the whole town knows those facts. I repeat, this crazy-mad person is not my friend. She can eat shit and die."

"Don't get your dander in a ball. I'm thinking she is off her rocker, too. The man only wants to talk to you."

Rowell contemplated the issue. "I have nothing to say."

The sheriff needed to explain the real visit. "One half of a wood coffin has appeared on a mound of sand in a marsh."

Rowell covered his surprise. "I'm not understanding what a coffin would have to do with anything. We have floodwaters all the time. The cheap coffins are made of wood. Wood floats. Am I missing something?"

"They found some bloodstains inside."

Rowell shook his head. "You are wondering if the blood is from Belinda."

The sheriff nodded. "From what I understand, the police couldn't find Belinda because there were no fingerprints nor DNA. Records got lost. It took them awhile to hook up Jane Doe to her."

Rowell thought about tenth grade.

"Her unsuccessful suicide attempts and the nursing home. Of course, they know her blood type from those records."

The sheriff saw Rowell was getting the picture.

"All I know is someone in town thought they saw her walking the beach a year ago. There was a couple who thought their sailboat was used. They complained about a bottle of missing pills. Belinda was into pills when she was in the nursing home. The nurse told us the patients complained about her stealing their tiny paper cups of pills. The nurses left the pills unattended because they were overloaded with work. Then one of the houses close to the pier was broken into by the railroad steps. That couple was missing pills."

"Great! Belinda, the killer, and drug addict were here or some other thief."

The sheriff was only delivering a message.

"Talk to the man. I would hate to see you leave. You're the only thing interesting happening in this small town. But I get there are more important things. We want you to be happy."

"Thanks, Bill. I'll talk to the investigator. I thought I saw Belinda once with my binoculars. The woman looked different. I tried to convince myself that she wasn't back. Now, I think I might have been mistaken."

The sheriff got up to leave. "Your tree has sunk in the backyard."

"I know. When I got my new tractor, I dug too deep. The fill I used was fluff. It occurred to me a red tree would look bright in the space. Wrong idea. Do you need a tree?"

"Heck, no. why would you buy a tree? The woods are full of them."

"This tree is red maple."

"Red maple, green maple, my answer is still no. Trees drop leaves. Leaves mean work. You could saw the sunken tree down."

The two men said their goodbyes.

Rowell met with the investigator. The investigator walked his property and asked about the landscaping changes. Rowell answered truthfully.

"I'm tired of mowing the grass."

All the handmade darts were burned up in Rowell's trash barrel. The wood was used to hold the cement for the new workshop floor. Then those wood pieces were burned. There was nothing on Rowell's property to implicate him in a crime.

His boat was spotless.

After the meeting with the investigator, Rowell knew he made the right choice. The investigator filled him in on the reign of terror that transpired. There would be no more horrible happenings from the likes of Belinda Cummings were Rowell's thoughts. He knew she was dead.

He wanted to shout with joy. Rowell was glad Amber was free from the woman's tyranny. Now Amber could live if she were still out there.

He took his boat fishing and watched the sunset. The water calmed his soul. He drove back to shore and started the winch to pull his boat onto the boat trailer.

Rowell pulled his boat and truck to one side of the road. He walked back to the boat ramp. Suddenly, he walked down the beach. People were outside laughing and cooking. He smelled hamburgers and occasionally fish.

There were a few bonfires. Children were searching for long sticks. The marshmallow bag sat in wait on the larger rocks. He knew the graham crackers and chocolate were guarded by the mothers.

He stopped. This was the way life should be. People were relaxing and having an enjoyable time. Rowell couldn't remember the last time that he enjoyed some fun. He remembered an image of a picnic long ago. The picnic was filled with food, laughter, and games.

He went back to his truck and drove home. He turned on the mermaid fountain. Then he remembered the best part. He was with Amber in his car on a moonlit night.

He loved Amber with all his heart. She was the only thing that mattered to him. One time she made a slip. She said Cara when talking about her mom.

Rowell decided to look up the name on the internet. He saw a child's name in the birth certificate records. He wondered. The child's name haunted him. Some force was working. He felt pushed to do more research.

There was more than one person who felt Amber was alive. He was one of those people who believed.

"Maybe I am wrong. There should be a body. There is no dead body. Amber vanished without a trace. Today, we are talking the impossible."

He corrected himself. People vanished every day.

Rowell drove to Minneapolis to a store that sold large fishing lures, rods, and reels with heavy lines. He bought stronger nets.

Driving back home, he applied for the next year's license and sent the documents to his printer.

The next spring, he went fishing in the same spot. His line was only fifty feet. He let the line go out. There was nothing. There were no massive fish or little fish. It was as if the place was a toxic wasteland.

"Oh, crap, I forgot about her plastic arm. That's why there are no fish."

Rowell beat his head with his hand.

"I should have removed her fake arm."

He sat there eating some chili and a cheese sandwich. The chili was slightly warm, and the cheese was still frozen. His boat floated some distance when he saw an object in the water. The boat drifted closer, and he looked at the object.

Jumping up, he threw the chili bowl and sandwich in the water. Rowell raced to the back of the boat and started his engine. He revved the boat so fast the front pulled out of the water.

Rowell eased back and felt relieved. The plastic was Belinda's fake arm. The body would eventually surface.

He never returned to the spot. The map and memory location were discarded.

HOPE FOR THE FUTURE

39 WEDDING INVITATION

Rowell read the wedding invitation. The person getting married was a name he didn't know. He racked his brain and couldn't bring up any image of the prospective bride or groom.

"This must be a joke."

He looked at the envelope again. The address was his address and name. He looked at the parent's name. He read, former *Trixie Moran.*

Then the name hit him.

"Trixie, the cheerleader, was Amber's friend. She was a great and sexy cheerleader from a competing team."

He fingered the RSVP. He indicated his answer was *yes* to both the wedding and reception. Rowell drove to Red Wing and dropped the envelope in the outside mailbox to make sure the invitation would be received. He walked up the steps and went inside the post office. He purchased some stamps.

Next was the drive to the small hardware store, and he bought a box of nails. Then he went to a restaurant downtown that served walleye sandwiches, batter fried. After eating his meal, he felt full and drove home.

Rowell would go to Eau Claire and buy something from the bride's gift registry. He was thinking sturdy silver stuff. Once inside the store, he almost fell over at the price of silver. He chose an expensive plate that looked like it might hold a loaf of bread.

Next, he went to a good men's clothing store where he was fitted for a new suit. He bought several shirts and ties. The man pointed him in the direction of the shoe store across the freeway.

Rowell bought new shoes for the event. Putting his packages in his car, he relaxed. The clothing store would mail him his altered suit.

Rowell drove home feeling good about the upcoming wedding. He knew the church and the hotel where the reception would be held. He made his reservations at the hotel. He was prepared.

Meanwhile, the Mississippi River barge worker saw a dead body in the barge's wake. He told the barge captain who slowed the rig. The emergency police boat arrived, retrieved the body, and the barge continued the rest of its journey. The body looked like the woman floated to the surface and rolled under the barge bottoms several times.

An autopsy was performed. There were puncture marks on the upper back torso. The police and investigators assumed the body belonged to Belinda Cummings. Based on the location and the last physical sighting, they knew she was dead some time ago. There was no explanation for the marks other than barges don't have smooth bottoms. The blood test match and missing arm confirmed their theory. The Belinda Cummings case was quickly and officially closed.

Rowell never went fishing again. He thought the water was polluted. He felt guilty.

"I should have buried her."

40 WEDDING RECEPTION

He took a second helping of roast beef and potatoes at the wedding reception and sat down at one of the tables.

Trixie's mother sat down next to him with a plate of wedding cake.

"You must be my daughter's friend from the other high school. How nice that you could come? I'm Stella."

Rowell shook her hand, "I'm Rowell Blackman."

She ate her wedding cake, and he finished his food.

"I'm glad to see someone enjoyed the meal. My ex-husband insisted on dinner. I made him pay for the entire wedding. Did you like the church ceremony?"

"Yes, the church is the perfect venue, the music was divine, and the minister talked too long."

Stella smiled.

"I've been married three times. You would think a person would learn. The minister was a little too gabby for my taste."

Rowell picked up on the three times.

"I suppose I should have tried marriage once. Then I might have some cool war stories to tell people."

Stella stared at him. She saw intelligence.

"I like you," Stella commented.

"I like you, too. You say what you want. Most people don't."

218

He was going to leave. Stella put her hand out.

"You should stay. There will be a dance in ten minutes. There are a lot of pretty young girls here."

She nodded toward some women congregating around the band players.

"You're correct. They are young."

"It doesn't matter. You don't have to marry them, just dance and enjoy yourself."

Rowell sat back down. Stella saw a faraway look in his eyes.

"My daughter, Trixie, used to look like you. She missed Amber so much."

"I wish Amber were here. I'd be a lot happier. Sometimes I see her walking in a field. Then Amber vanishes in a mist or cloud. I realize my mind has played tricks on me. You would think I would learn."

He stopped. "I'm sorry. This reception is your family's time to play and party."

"Sometimes dreams come true. We never know the future. We can only hope."

Rowell sighed, "I've wished and hoped so much, the sky must be filled with a million words."

"The sky picture is delightful. About six months after Amber disappeared, Trixie changed. She stopped worrying about Amber. There was a smile on her face."

"She stopped wishing."

Stella needed to give the man some advice.

"My daughter is special. Amber is special. Keep the faith."

The music started playing.

"Rowell, please dance with me one dance. I want my friends to see that I can find a good-looking younger man. I'll be the talk of their gossip parties for weeks."

Rowell stood and held out his hand. He danced three dances with Stella before an older gentleman interrupted him. The young girls didn't waste a moment to grab his hand for the next dances.

After an hour, he told them he must stop and get a drink. Rowell took a glass of champagne off one of the trays on the table. He took a sip.

Trixie stood next to him with her glass. "Rowell, the amazing quarterback, I'm glad you came. How about a toast?"

He held his glass next to hers.

"To Amber and our forever friendship."

Rowell was surprised.

"To Amber and your lovely daughter. May there only be joy in their future."

They clinked glasses.

"Very nice wedding. I was not sure about coming, but I am glad you asked me. Your name took a while to put with a face. See, the football players did notice the opposing team's cheerleaders, especially the super ones."

She grinned. "Yes, being a super cheerleader was great. However, I was hoping that a friend of mine would appear. She must have changed her mind."

"Ah, this invitation was supposed to be a setup."

Trixie looked apologetic. "I was trying to help a friend."

"That's okay, Trixie, I'm doing fine. I have a boat now."

"You must like to go fishing?"

His eyes crinkled, "I used to like to go fishing. Now I order fish in restaurants. I thank you for a fun evening. Tell Stella that I enjoyed dancing with her very much. Your mother is wise. She made me feel better. Goodnight, Trixie."

"I will let her know. Goodnight."

Trixie watched him leave the hall. She thought he looked lonely. Trixie moved to talk with her mother.

41 ANACORTES

Rowell looked out the airplane window and saw the Seattle runway below. The passengers would be departing the airplane soon. Their flight made up for the time delay in the air and landed on time.

He joined the throng of passengers grabbing their luggage from the overhead bins. The plane emptied slowly. Rowell held his small suitcase and briefcase and finally entered the airport. He looked for the signs and turned to follow the others toward the terminal and food.

Finding a teriyaki place, he selected a seafood rice bowl and hot tea. The food court was full of people. He moved over to let a woman sit down. She asked him where he was going.

"Anacortes."

"Good choice. You should take the ferry to one of the islands. Then you can see the Seattle area."

"Where are you going?"

"I have friends in Seattle, and then I'm going to Vancouver."

"Isn't Vancouver northwest of Anacortes?"

"Yes, as the crow flies. I must go. My friend sent me a text that she is in the parking facility."

Rowell waved to her and finished his meal. He went to the car rental agency and picked up his vehicle. He made sure the vehicle contained GPS. He entered the address and drove to the building.

Walking inside, he talked with the clerk.

222

"I'm looking for some information. A friend of mine disappeared. Her mother, Cara Manus used to live here. She died in a climbing accident and left behind a daughter named Catherine Anne. I saw the child's name on your website. I know Cara had a boyfriend."

The clerk nodded. "I remember reading about Cara Manus."

Encouraged by her words, he continued.

"I don't know the boyfriend's name. I'm taking a leap of faith that he signed Catherine Anne's birth certificate as the father. Would you be able to tell me his name?"

The clerk bit her lower lip. "I'm not supposed to divulge information."

"You could write the name on a piece of paper and accidentally leave it on the counter. Please, this is important. He's the missing link to finding Catherine Anne."

"Just a minute." The clerk disappeared and came back with a yellow sticky. She handed him the paper.

"Thank you from the bottom of my heart."

The clerk brought up a copy of the phone directory and shoved the book in his direction. He didn't find the young man's name but did find the last name that matched. He wrote down the address and left the building.

Finding the clapboard blue home, Rowell saw the grass was high. He knocked on the door, and no one answered, so he went towards the back door. An elderly gentleman was sitting on the cement steps.

Rowell joined him. "Hello, sir, your lawn needs mowing."

"The lawnmower won't start. My son used to fix things."

"Where is your lawnmower?" The man pointed toward the garage.

"Do you mind if I take a look?"

"No. Go right ahead."

Rowell stepped into the garage and turned the light on. He found the lawnmower and saw the frayed cord. Looking around the shop, he found some rope of comparable size and tools. He brought the lawnmower outside and proceeded to take it apart. He fixed the rope and took the blade off. Rowell sharpened the blade and put the lawnmower back together. The man continued smoking his pipe while watching Rowell.

He filled the tank with gasoline and dumped a small can of oil in one place. He pulled a few times on the cord, and the engine started. Rowell mowed the old man's yard in between sneezes. When he was done. He turned the mower over and cleared the blades of debris.

After placing the mower back inside the garage, he sat down. The old man looked at him and nodded. Rowell blew his nose.

"I do have some questions about your son's daughter named Catherine Anne. I know Connie and Cyrus Wood."

"Cyrus passed away quite a while ago."

"Yes, I know. I'm trying to find Catherine Anne. I must speak to her."

"She was a pretty little thing. Skinny as a rail. Cyrus came with legal papers. He did ask our permission. My wife couldn't take care of the child nor my son. We didn't mind when he took her away. We knew she would have a better life in Minneapolis."

"How old was Catherine Anne when Cyrus took her?"

"She must have been five years old."

Rowell processed the information.

"Did the Wood's adopt Catherine Anne Manus?"

"Don't rightly know."

Rowell rubbed his face. "They changed her name to Amber."

"Pretty name."

Rowell looked at the freshly mowed lawn and sneezed.

"Have you seen her recently?"

The man looked at his yard.

"Now that the lawnmower works, the neighbor boy will mow for me. I appreciate your helping us. My wife is in the house. She can sleep through a tornado."

Rowell was almost finished with his visit. He needed answers.

"Amber. Was she here?"

"No, not after my son was arrested, but maybe later."

Rowell's eyes watered.

"Catherine Anne visited us maybe twenty years ago. She told me she was going to study medicine. She wanted to be a doctor or teach medicine, I think."

"I can see her being a teacher. She was kind and patient."

"We did get a few cards. The city was Vancouver. I don't remember the addresses. She moved around. I should have sent her a note. She stopped writing."

Rowell felt relief and apprehension. He didn't have a passport. He would need to go home.

Rowell stood up, and he helped the old man up the steps to his back door.

"You take care of yourself, young man."

He watched the old man enter his house. Rowell stepped into his rental car and drove to the hotel. In the evening he walked down to the ferry landing and watched the cars and passengers exit and board.

His return ticket was for tomorrow evening. He would go to the Seattle airport and take an earlier flight home.

There were new plans for his future.

42 SOLD HOME

The realtor told her client the good news.

"They want the furniture and landscape ornaments included in the sale. They would like to purchase your tractor and boat. My clients don't want woodworking equipment."

Rowell looked at the prices.

"You can write up the contract. I need two months. I have a friend who will buy my woodworking equipment and tools."

The realtor left, and Rowell ordered the boxes he would need from an online vendor. He contacted the leasing agent and sent her a deposit and check for the house in Canada. He was waiting for his passport to arrive.

He saw the sheriff's car parked out front. The man carried a small box.

"I went to Wabasha and got us some good donuts and rolls. You still know how to make coffee?"

"Come in, Bill. I appreciate you buying breakfast this time. The coffee pot is fresh. I'll get us cups and plates."

The two men sat down and ate in silence.

"The whole town is going to miss you, boy. We're used to seeing your truck around town. No, sir, things will never be the same when our quarterback leaves."

Rowell patted the sheriff on the shoulder.

"I'll be back on occasion. You haven't seen the last of me. Tell them they aren't getting rid of me. I know my roots."

The sheriff grinned and ate his jelly donut.

"I'm glad you will be back. You stop and see me before you leave."

"I will."

Two months later Rowell was in a tiny house in Vancouver. His boxes were stacked in the living room. A sleeping bag was on the floor in the bedroom. The room would only be able to handle a twin bed.

"What have I done?"

He looked at the walls of the kitchen. The paint was peeling off the ceiling.

"There must be a leak in the roof. There's an old ladder in the garage. I should look. First, there is something more important to do."

Every morning at seven-thirty, he bought a cup of coffee and scone from the coffee shop in the building next to where Dr. Catherine A. Manus lived. He didn't see her.

Rowell wondered if he made a mistake moving here before contacting her. He finally went to the college buildings where she taught school.

He talked to a person in the administration building.

"The school is on spring break. This year the break is three weeks. Most of the instructors leave the area. I imagine Dr. Manus has done the same. The answer is no. We can't give out the information about her home."

Rowell felt sick to his stomach. She might be anywhere. He would need to wait a little more. He went back to the rental and climbed on the roof. Finding the missing roof tile spots, he looked in the garage. The few tiles were brittle.

"The whole roof is going to disintegrate on this house."

He talked to the landlord who would only pay for repairs if Rowell would do them. He drove to the store and bought some shingles and black gook.

In three days, the roof was better and should last a little longer. He cleaned his hands and threw the gook can in the garbage. The rest of the new shingles were put in the garage. He bought some paint for the kitchen and paint supplies. Then he ran out of steam.

Rowell went into town and found a pub that served tuna fish sandwiches. The tuna was a large chunk of whole meat and not from a can. He took his sandwich and drink outside and watched the water. Several ships and ferries went by. He looked at his calendar.

"One more week, and I will get to see her."

Rowell rehearsed his lines over, and over again. He could imagine her taking him into her waiting arms.

"What if things don't go that way? You need to be prepared. Her world is different now."

He worried that Amber changed.

"I've changed. My hair is thinner. Then there's the other problem. I will need to explain the accident. What if she won't forgive me?"

Rowell left some pieces of bread for the birds and walked down to the wharf. He walked inside her building and asked at the guard desk if Dr. Manus was in. They told him she was not.

He walked back to an ice cream shop and selected the hand-formed marionberry ice cream. After eating the last bite of a cookie-rolled cone, he went to his car and drove home.

"If she hates me, I will go back home and live with my friend in his apartment until I find a place. But his feet stink. Rowell, you'll buy a can of air freshener."

Rowell remembered the last time they talked. His conversation with Amber was short. They were both abrupt with each other. He paced the kitchen and stopped. There was something he forgot, but he couldn't quite put his finger on it.

"Think, man. What did you forget?"

He opened his computer and checked his bank account. The money from the sale of his home and private property was in his account. His money was safe. He received a new driver's license and paid for new license plates. His passport was good. His boxes arrived safely. There were new checks from the newly opened bank account in his duffel bag.

He ticked the items off his list. The address change came through, and he was receiving the final bills from Pepin. He wrote those checks and put stamps on the envelopes. Walking to the mailbox on the corner, he placed the letters inside.

Still, his brain was flickering.

"I've been so busy lately. My excitement is mounting from the additional wait time to see Amber or Catherine. Stress, that's the problem. I'm obsessing again. Stop it, Rowell. Don't blow this thing!"

He felt a little better. The paint can he opened with a screwdriver. He never thought he would have to paint walls as a renter. The place looked brighter. He was pleased with himself. Rowell washed the brush and put the paint lid back on the can.

"I should write something on the wall. This wall needs words."

Crawling on top of his sleeping bag, he fell into a dead-like sleep.

The next morning, he went back to the store and bought stencils, black paint, and blue masking tape. He found a level in one of the mover boxes and some chalk string.

He taped the stencils to the wall along the level chalk line. Carefully, he painted and let the black paint dry. He removed the stencils and stood back.

Sometimes Dreams Come True.

"The words fit the wall perfectly."

43 RENEE'S MEETING

The housekeeper ushered Renee into Cyrus's old library. She sat in a black leather chair and looked at the bookcases of old and new books. Mrs. Wood was out for the morning getting her hair done.

Catherine walked into the room. Renee arose, and they shook hands. The seventeen-year-old girl grew into an elegant and regal woman. Renee was thrilled to meet the main and significant character of her book.

"Should I call you Amber or Catherine?"

"Catherine, please."

"Can you tell me why you disappeared?"

Catherine looked at the stacks of books on the floor.

"My father loved this room. I'm pulling the older books. One of the libraries is interested in my donation and ancient books. He would be pleased. In answer to your question. I was a minor, and I did what my father thought was best. I understand my mother showed you my collection."

"Now you are older and could reveal yourself. Belinda is officially dead. I liked the amber specimens and jewelry."

"Which piece did you like?"

Renee thought about the mosquitos and bees.

"I especially liked the red amber heart bracelet. I'm a bracelet person, although yellow is my favorite."

Catherine stood up.

"My father told me his heart would always be mine after my mother, of course. She has an even larger red heart and a wider cuff bracelet. He bought us the red amber presents for Valentine's Day one year and surprised us both."

Catherine looked at the ceiling and shook her head.

"My lawyer has given me his advice regarding any revelation about my identity. I should heed his warning. You have been a nice person to Trixie, my mother, and Mrs. Abrams plus you are writing a fiction book. I'll try to be frank with you."

"You disappeared because you and your parents were frightened for your safety."

"Yes, I believe that I heard Bev murdered by Belinda. I was supposed to be at the same party. I hid under a boat when I realized not many people were there. Belinda was a cheerleader who somehow disliked the world and me. Therefore, I was cautious. Not revealing myself might have saved my life."

Renee wondered, "Why was she angry?"

Catherine raised her hands in dismay. "Perhaps Belinda was angry with Bev that I never showed. They argued. The police found Bev's body someplace different. If I showed my face, I think Belinda would have blamed me for her death or killed me instead. My dad believes that I was the original target at the beach party. I agreed with him."

"Why did you go, and why would Belinda want to harm you? She was just a teenager."

"Age doesn't matter with her type of personality. As a young person, she was dangerous. She needed to hate someone. I was different and rich. Her father's business failed. I had everything. Belinda also stole something precious from my home. She offered to give the object back. I think she lied about most everything."

Renee could see the reason for the jealousy. "Belinda wanted what you had? Of course, she did. She stole your yellow-amber ball. The ball was your first gift from Connie and Cyrus. The ball meant that you were well-loved."

"At least, Bev hinted at something Belinda wanted to return to me. There was a male who was there and left. I'm not sure if it was Alec Rivers. I did become suspicious of him before the beach party. Our first meeting with each other seemed odd. His being at the game seemed even stranger. I think he knew Belinda early on and might have been in some relationship, but I can't be sure. Now we will never know."

Renee knew Alec was also a target.

"You let Trixie know that you were alive. Why didn't you tell Rowell?"

"My father thought the fewer people that knew I was alive, the better. I agreed with him. I might have placed Rowell in jeopardy. We weren't exactly sociable when I left."

"You know Rowell talks about you. When I interviewed him recently, I gathered there were still strong feelings on his part. He is a person who believes you will one day reappear."

234

Catherine seemed visibly upset. Renee thought her next comments were out of character.

"Rowell should stop believing in the impossible. Amber's not going to return."

Renee wasn't sure Catherine knew her former boyfriend was a hero.

"Rowell was on two tours for the military for this country. He has won prestigious medals. Rowell would welcome being in danger and can take care of bad people."

Catherine frowned.

"Belinda reached Alec. She could easily have done the same to Rowell. Men act strong. The enemy is like an angry dinosaur come back to life."

Renee knew Catherine was getting defensive and worried. This was not what she wanted to accomplish at this interview.

"Belinda is gone, and the danger has probably disappeared. My book is almost finished. I need to know if you would like Amber to remain missing?"

Catherine hesitated and walked down an aisle of books. She touched the binding of a book.

"My life revolves around Catherine now. My colleagues and students know me. No one knows Amber. Amber is gone. I would like her to remain a mystery."

"What about Agnes? She talked about you."

Catherine looked embarrassed. "Yes, I'll see her before I leave and explain. She will be okay with my current name and life. She's been a faithful servant to my parents."

Renee nodded.

"I'll send you a pre-author copy. Please read the book and let me know if I should change or publish the story."

Catherine stood up. "Thank you. I'm sure the book will be a good one."

The housekeeper appeared. Renee knew their interview was over. Catherine walked with her to the foyer.

Renee held out her hand. Catherine surprised her with a hug.

"Be safe," said Renee.

Renee went to her truck and drove to the cabin. Her husband was waiting when she opened the door.

"Well, what did she say?"

Renee petted the dog and went to the refrigerator to make a sandwich. "The woman in my story will stay missing. I will honor her wishes as best I can."

"There goes your romantic part of the story."

She sat down at the table.

"Yes, totally trashed the long, lost lover's theory. I should write paranormal stuff in the future. An author can let their imagination run wild."

Her husband rubbed her shoulders. "You would make a good paranormal writer. That's like science fiction, right?"

"Dodo, do, do!"

"Hey, I understand. This story is nuttier than the fruitcake you make at Christmastime. Did you know there's only one loaf left? Hint, hint! This Belinda

236

person was a psycho who lived in her scary world. She needed dead bodies to fuel her brain. We should be glad someone stopped her from killing people who loved Amber."

She thought about her husband's last three sentences. "You are correct," said Renee.

Her husband hugged his wife.

"Who ate all the fruitcake?" she asked.

Renee went into the blue bedroom and opened her notebook computer. She clicked on the story and started a new chapter. When she finished the chapter, she stopped. No words were swirling in her writer's brain. She talked to the dog.

"I lost my train of thought. We might as well go for a walk."

The dog's ears perked up, and he jumped off the small navy-blue couch. There was a knock at the door. The dog raced to the door and started barking at two boys holding a bag of apples.

The two boys bent and petted their dog when she opened the door. She stepped outside.

"Hello, Henri and Rob. You rode a long way on your bikes."

Henri was grinning. "I have a new bike with gears like Rob. The gears make riding easier. We stopped at Mrs. Abrams' old house. They let us pick apples from her orchard."

Rob extended the bag and spoke.

"We saw your flowers and name card. You liked Mrs. Abrams, too."

"I did. Thanks for the apples. My husband loves pie. The dog does as well."

The two boys left, and she put the apples on the kitchen counter.

"I'll help peel the apples," offered her husband.

She took the stick of butter out of the freezer.

"I needed those boys to stop today. They cheered me out of my writer's block."

"Good. Do you want thick chunks?"

"No, I'll slice them once the apples are quartered."

They worked together to get the pie made and in the oven.

"Did you know Rowell sold his house and moved?"

Renee stopped. "How do you know, and where did he go?"

"I stopped in town and filled the gas tank on the truck. His friend was at the other gas pump and recognized me. Rowell talked about us. His friend even knew where the cabin was located. He mentioned there were turkeys in the front field. He told me Rowell sold everything in Pepin and moved to Vancouver."

Renee set the timer on the stove.

"The story has stepped up a notch. Good for Rowell. He figured out where Catherine lived. I wonder if my ending will change."

44 STRANGER THINGS

The people in the coffee shop in Vancouver were extra noisy. Rowell lifted his coffee in the air to squeeze past a patron. He bumped into Catherine's arm.

"Sorry, today is busy. Everyone wants coffee."

He looked at the beautiful woman about thirty-eight years old dressed in a business suit. She was directly in front of him. Her light brown hair still showed highlights. The highlights were from a beauty shop.

She turned, and his heart stopped. Amber was older, but he would know her anywhere. There was a flicker of recognition in her eyes. He followed her outside.

Exasperatedly, she asked, "Rowell, what are you doing here?"

"Buying coffee?"

She was angry with him. "You shouldn't be here."

"I live in a rental in town. I figured out your new name, and I wanted to see you. I missed Amber, and now I've found her."

"My name is Catherine. Amber is gone. She belongs to the past."

Rowell stepped aside to let someone move around them.

"I have to go. My new classes start today."

"When can I see you? We can go to dinner somewhere. Anywhere would be okay with me."

"I don't think that is a very good idea."

Now Rowell was angry. She was giving him the brushoff. "No, you don't. I need some answers. We were friends once. We were more than friends. You kissed me like you meant what you said. We loved each other once. You owe me an explanation."

Catherine did owe him a response. "My father helped me disappear. There's your answer. He and my mother protected me."

"That's it?"

Catherine started walking to her building's underground parking. He followed her like a puppy. She relented.

"Here's my card. I'm free Tuesday at about six in the evening. We'll grab something on the wharf to eat. You are right. We must talk."

He took her business card and watched her walk away. He drank his lukewarm coffee and sat at a small table. He talked to himself.

"Well, our meeting went wrong. I hadn't expected a cold reaction. Rowell, you thought about this meeting long and hard. You shouldn't have surprised her."

Rowell rubbed his forehead. "You're an idiot."

He went back to his rental and chipped at the ceiling. "I need some filler."

He drove to the hardware store, bought spackle plaster in a tub, and drove to the tiny house. Rowell smeared the stuff on as smoothly as he could. He forgot to buy sandpaper. He made another trip to the store to get the sandpaper. The clerk looked at him strangely.

"Look, I forgot the sandpaper. People forget stuff. Wait until you are my age."

Rowell went grumpily back to the rental. "This place is a dump. Catherine lives in an expensive high rise. She won't be impressed."

The evening arrived. He showered and shaved and drove to town. He parked in guest parking in her building and went to the front desk. She was waiting for him.

They ate dinner on the wharf. He couldn't remember what he ordered. The food tasted like crab, but he wasn't sure. They strolled down the walkway.

"Mint?"

Rowell took two mints from the tiny metal can, and he chewed them.

"I looked for you forever. I drove to Minneapolis hoping to find you. My life stopped when you disappeared. I joined the military hoping that I would catch a bullet."

"Oh, Rowell, you were always dramatic."

The conversation was headed again in the wrong direction. "You used to say that I was funny and strong."

"You are strong. I owe you my life. I know you got the best of Belinda."

Rowell was amazed at her perception. "Belinda came after me with a stolen gun. She gave me no choice. I was better prepared."

"When I read about the pricks to her body, I remembered the tiny dart box you made."

He watched the lights inside the ferry as it went past. "I forgot about the box."

Catherine touched his cheek. "It's okay, Rowell. I won't ever tell. We are friends."

Rowell took a step toward her and kissed her gently on the lips. She didn't move. He kissed her a second time. Catherine pulled away.

"I can't do us, again."

"How do you know? I just got here. We can move slow. Your future is free. I'm a free man. There's nothing to be afraid of. The monster is gone."

"Why didn't you fight for me in eleventh grade?"

Rowell was confused. "What are you talking about? I wanted you."

"No, you let Alec take over."

"I believed that you wanted him."

Catherine rolled her eyes. "I didn't. You guessed wrong."

He was aghast. His voice rose. "You're telling me this now!"

She angrily stared at him. "Don't holler at me. How could I tell you? Belinda was out there. I felt sure she would find me. Her ways were so evil."

He didn't know what to say. He was thinking back to when his life changed. "I was inexperienced. You were the same. Our youth didn't help much."

She remembered.

"I was trying to be cool. Somehow, being cool didn't work," replied Catherine.

He took her hands. She pulled away from him. There was a coldness in her voice.

"Give me some time."

Rowell looked at the dark water. He wondered if there were any gigantic fish near the surface. He thought about the whale who ate some person. He remembered the person was Joshua from the Bible story. He should have fallen on his knees or something. She was going to walk away. The girl he once knew was better older, wiser, and more educated. She saw things clearer. She wouldn't take any more chances.

He needed to convince her. Now was not good. Rowell knew this woman was different. She was stronger.

He thought he saw an Orca laughing at him in the water. Years of stress were taking hold. His stomach didn't feel well. It was jumping and sloshing.

"Here's my address. The house is tiny and a mess. If you like to paint, come, and join me some day or evening. Daytime is better."

Rowell turned his coat collar to stop the wind, and he walked away. After a block, he increased the pace. Then he started running. Grabbing his door open, he barely made the bathroom. He put his head in his hands.

"Why didn't I tell her how much love there was for us in my heart?"

Catherine watched him go. She thought about what he told her. She was still afraid. All these years, she was like one of the bugs trapped inside a piece of yellow amber in her collection. She was afraid for so many years, she didn't know how to live. Change for her was difficult.

"Where to begin?"

She shouldn't have asked him about fighting for her. Tears touched her eyes. She had hurt Rowell once again. He was the last person she wanted to hurt or destroy. She needed to get her head on straight. Their accidental meeting was a shock.

"He's still a good kisser."

She would make her decision in a week. There were teacher workshops at the end of next week. Catherine didn't need the extra credit. She could spend time with Rowell if she wanted. The choice was hers.

She walked back to her apartment.

"We've been apart years yet today was like time stood still. I was in yesterday. I was in Rowell's arms. I didn't want to leave. I shouldn't have disappeared."

Catherine knew she would be dead if she had stayed.

"The future is what I want. Pretty soon, I will retire from teaching. I don't want to be alone. My mother hates her loneliness. Rowell has opened a door that I thought didn't exist. He has offered me freedom."

She remembered his comment about why he went into the military. She was glad he didn't catch a bullet.

"Trixie, I should have come to your daughter's wedding. You kept encouraging me to be spontaneous and change my life. You will be amazed that Rowell is at my doorstep. The writer also wanted romance for her book, love everlasting."

244

She looked at the address on the paper in her pocket. She put the address on her navigation App. The house was in a poorer neighborhood.

The next weekend, Catherine made her decision and drove to the address. She sat in her car.

"I should go in."

She re-started her car, and after a minute turned the engine off. Catherine looked at the front door. She walked the broken narrow sidewalk to the house. She hesitated.

There was a screen door between her and Rowell. She pushed on the screen and stopped. She knocked on the chipped screen door.

"Come in. Don't touch the walls."

His hands were dripping with paint from the roller. He saw his visitor, stepped away, and threw the roller in the sink.

Hastily Rowell scrubbed his hands and grabbed a towel to dry. He rushed to her side. He realized she was only two feet inside the rental. He held her tight.

There were no words. They kissed for a long time. He led her into the kitchen. She looked around.

"You will leave this horrible place and live with me until we can decide what to do about us. I do like the black words on the wall."

Rowell was ecstatic. "There is us like in a couple?"

"Yes."

He hugged her and saw the blue suits of police officers at his front door. Rowell released her as one of the policemen opened the screen door. There was a man from the FBI he recognized.

"Rowell Blackman, you are under arrest for the murder of Cyrus Wood. The people who bought your home found the gun under the floorboards. They turned the gun into the local sheriff while I was visiting him. Sheriff Edwards didn't have a choice. I took the gun as potential evidence. The ballistics match the bullet that killed Mr. Wood."

Catherine's eyes were large, and her face was white. Rowell struggled against the officers who grabbed his arms.

"It was an accident, I swear."

Rowell was looking at Catherine.

"I was going to tell you. I couldn't. We were finding our way. The gun is old, and the safety was loose. Your dad surprised me. I was watching your house. I wanted to make sure you were safe."

The police dragged him away. Catherine sat in one of his kitchen chairs. She believed him.

She dialed her lawyer and the college. She would not be teaching this semester.

45 LITTLE TIME BEFORE THE TRIAL

Rowell watched as a stranger approached. He was sitting in a jail cell. The man handed him his card.

"My firm has been hired to defend you. We have offices in Minneapolis. For now, Dr. Manus has paid your bail. Canada will take several months to do the paperwork to transfer the case back to the United States."

"Is Catherine outside?"

"I have warned my client that you could be a flight risk."

"Don't worry, I'm not going anywhere. You have given me about three months to live the life I always wanted. Catherine is everything. I won't disappoint her."

The jailer unlocked the cell. His lawyer walked with him to the outside of the building. Rowell looked at the blue sky. A person didn't appreciate freedom until the bars or fear were removed.

Catherine was waiting in a taxi. Rowell climbed inside and squeezed her hand. He was afraid to hug or kiss her.

The taxi stopped in the circular drive. She paid for the taxi. He let her lead and followed her to the elevator of her building.

When they reached the tenth floor, they went to her apartment. She unlocked the door, and they stepped inside.

"Your keys are on the counter. I'll order some takeout. Tomorrow we can get groceries."

She made the call to the restaurant. Rowell walked around the plush rooms. He came back into the kitchen.

"This is a very nice apartment, or should I say impressive, like its owner?"

"The building security people are also nice. I informed them of your situation. My lawyer will defend you. I believe my father's shooting was an accident. There is no way you could have known his car would break down. He never walked. In India, we waited half an hour for rickshaws. The shop was a short distance. My father shouldn't have been walking in Minneapolis. He was ill. No, he was extremely ill with cancer."

"I appreciate your hiring a legal team. I have money and will pay you back. I'm sorry your dad was ill."

"This is not about money. I could care less. I don't want you to go to jail because of my family. I'm paying you back for protecting me from a psycho. It's my turn."

The food arrived, and they ate the pork chops and stuffing. He toyed with the green beans. There was a cake dessert.

"Coffee?"

"Sure."

"My bedroom is a white and gold room. Your bedroom is the one with a silver bedspread."

Rowell came over to Catherine. He made her stop with the cleanup from their meal. He took her into his arms and kissed her more passionately. She was surprised by his passion.

"Our bedroom is the gold one."

She started to object.

"You don't get to win this argument."

"We really shouldn't sleep together."

Rowell knew she liked to argue. She would need more persuasion. He kissed her longer.

"We've got three months before they might send me to jail. I'm not going to waste a moment. We've already let half our lifetime disappear due to a misunderstanding. I love you yesterday, today, tomorrow, and whatever comes after tomorrow."

Catherine shouldn't argue with him. He must understand her stance.

"They won't put you in jail. I'm sure they won't."

"Get real. I'm a jerk from a small town who used an old gun to kill someone rich and important. A jury is not going to be sympathetic when the opposing side shows them my military career. I should have known better."

She liked his firm body next to hers.

"We'll need to change the small-town look," suggested Catherine.

Rowell grinned. "Okay, my history should be disclosed before we get further distracted. I've had some relationships with women. Usually, they were short-lived. Your turn."

Catherine looked him in the eyes.

249

"I dated a professor for three years. We broke things off two years ago. There's been no one since."

"I thought I saw an Orca the other night in the water."

She laughed. "Really? There shouldn't be one in the location where we walked."

"We've cleared the air; what side of the bed do you want to sleep on?"

She started laughing harder.

"Rowell, we did a big reveal, and you are trying to figure out the bed arrangements?"

Rowell began laughing. He was being too serious.

"I see your point. I want us to go smoothly. It shouldn't matter. We have other things to worry about like birth control."

"I'm covered." His eyes lit up. He poured the strong coffee with frothy foam and sprinkled cinnamon on top.

"The good news is that I'm bare like the Orca. A little furry, too. I don't have any clothes."

He handed her the steaming cup.

"I don't mind furry. To us and winning the case!"

She toasted, and they both drank the hot liquid. Catherine would wait to tell him in the morning. His clothes were in the building in a storage locker.

The couple moved toward the bedroom. Rowell put his cup down on the nightstand and threw back the exquisite covers. The design was a long colorful totem pole on one side.

250

"Is this silk?"

Catherine nodded.

"Mostly silk and some other blends."

He laid down on the firm and comfortable mattress. She sat on the edge of the bed.

"My back was killing me. Do you know how hard linoleum can be? The rocks in Lake Superior are softer."

"My bed mattress is better. There is a button to change the angles. Wait until you see the six-headed shower. It's like running through a water fountain. Only the shower water is warm."

He turned to his side.

"The shower sounds manly and heavenly. Speaking of heaven, please come closer. Your hunk of a man is waiting."

"Hunk? Where do you get these nutty ideas?"

His eyes sparkled more.

"I was a star quarterback. You girls called us hunks when you thought we weren't listening."

She kicked her shoes off and slid closer. He unbuttoned her black silk blouse and undid the lacy black strapless bra.

"Nice underwear."

"Women call them lingerie."

"I have wanted to do this from the moment we met. You were very disciplined."

"Four of us cheerleaders made a pact to drive the boys crazy. The pact was Star's idea. Her father was as strict as mine."

He pulled her closer and kissed her again. She was wonderfully soft. He touched her hair.

"I like the highlights."

Catherine liked his eyes. She wanted to know.

"Happy, now?"

He watched her face. "Not yet. There's more to explore."

She moved away from him for a minute. He let her go. She selected a button on a different remote. The bedroom lights dimmed, and soft music came on over the hidden sound system.

Catherine slid towards her old friend.

"I have a waffle iron to the left of the stove."

Rowell smiled. "Come here, my delicious woman who tastes of cinnamon. I'll make you the best waffles in the world. First, we have to get through this romantic evening."

"Romantic? I remember some romantic words you tried to whisper in my ear," said Catherine.

"I'm beyond believable."

"Yes, you do remember."

The two lovers disappeared under the silk sheets and covers until morning. He sometimes used the wrong name. She didn't mind.

Rowell stumbled out of bed and went into the kitchen. The time was six o'clock in the morning. He found the bacon, eggs, flour, and milk. He saw the orange juice carton and found the coffee pods. He played with the coffee machine until the device started.

By the time Catherine opened her eyes, she smelled the food. Turning over she saw the food tray filled with a hot breakfast for two. There was a frozen strawberry on top of the stack of waffles. Rowell was in his underwear.

She tapped the strawberry. "Rock hard."

"Are you talking about me?"

She cut the waffle and dipped the slice in the small dish of syrup. Catherine held out the bite to him.

"You go ahead. I've already devoured my waffles. However, I'll eat my eggs and bacon."

He wolfed down the food. "I'm going to try your shower. Don't take too long eating."

"There's a large soap bar under the sink."

Catherine kept eating her breakfast. Finally, he went into the master bathroom. She could hear him singing off-key. She shouted at him.

"Your voice is terrible!"

She didn't hear him. The food tray was put aside, and she was going to get out of bed. Suddenly, he picked her up and carried her into the shower.

"You're all wet!"

"Tell me you like my voice."

She kept saying, "I've got to go to the bathroom."

"Promise me, you'll come back."

"Yes."

He let her go and counted out loud.

"Women take forever. I'm already at twenty-five."

She re-emerged and picked up the soap. He kissed her wet face.

Both knew their living arrangements would need some work to get the kinks out.

46 IN BETWEEN

The couple took every opportunity they could to spend time together. Their confidence and love grew. They went to the art galleries and took pictures of the suspension bridge in Vancouver. Museums filled the days and theaters filled part of their nights. Finding tasty food was one of Rowell's favorite outings. They bicycled in a large park and took a seaplane tour.

The time came for them to seriously think about the approaching court date in Minneapolis.

An expensive suit and more expensive shirts and shoes were required. Rowell looked at the price tags on the suits, and Catherine dragged him into the changing room. The sales clerk brought a large rack of suits for him to try on. Three other clerks brought him trays of elegant handkerchiefs, ties, and belts.

She sent him to an expensive barber for a haircut and shave. Catherine wanted Rowell to look like a million bucks when he was in court.

The small-town image wouldn't do to win over the jury. He needed to look like a professional businessman. They formed their corporation in Minnesota, and he was listed as president. Their firm was a woodworking business. She bought him a building and a brand-new manufacturing shop. He selected commercial equipment and fixtures.

Rowell wasn't sure what they were going to make. He started drawing designs with some new computer software.

Both wrote personal letters to their friends requesting their support during this challenging time. Rowell professed that he was innocent and explained in detail the fault of the old gun, his overwrought state of no sleep, and his error in judgment at leaving Cyrus's dead body. He did go to a phone booth to call in the emergency.

Rowell put a personal note to his friends that he found the love of his life. He didn't tell them her name. There was time for more information later.

They traveled two weeks early to Minneapolis. Mrs. Wood was delighted to have Rowell in her house. She forgave him because he loved her daughter.

The trial wasn't going so well despite five hundred signatures from the people from his old town. They claimed he was their hero.

The jury looked bored and unimpressed. They put Connie Wood on the stand, and the jury listened, but there was no change in their expressions. The defense argued Rowell's parent's house was old. People put things under the floor. The gun under the floor was normal.

Catherine knew that if she didn't do something, her potential fiancée was going to sit in prison for a long time. She told Rowell she needed an hour with her lawyers. Rowell went home with Mrs. Wood.

In the car ride, Mrs. Wood told him to drop the formality. He could call her Connie.

"When are you going to marry my daughter? I know you sneak into her room at night. We have hallway cameras, you know. I'm old, but not senile."

Rowell chuckled.

"I've asked her maybe fifty times. She wants to wait."

"My daughter is stubborn. Ask her once more. Tell her that I encouraged you. I would like to see my daughter married before I die."

"I love her very much."

"Rowell don't tell me. I can see your heart spilling out whenever she walks into the room. I'm not blind either. Go tell her a thousand times that you love her. You must make her see how serious you are."

"I know, but I'm not good at conversation."

"Don't be absurd. My husband courted me with flowers and worldly presents along with the sweet talk."

Rowell looked at Mrs. Wood.

"Connie, your husband was exceptional. I'm just this guy."

"Now you are being stupid. Rowell. I knew you when you were in high school. You were exceptional and a good athlete. My husband told me. The sheriff told me that you help little old ladies cross the street. Start believing in yourself."

They arrived at Connie's house.

"What do you think Catherine wants to talk about with the lawyers?"

The woman was helped from the car by her nurse.

"She will reveal all."

Rowell walked into the house and waited in the library for Catherine.

When she appeared and told him her plan. He argued with her. She wouldn't budge from her decision.

"Your mother told me you were stubborn."

"She is a fine one to accuse me."

Rowell was trying to rethink his comeback. "I love you a thousand, gad-zillion times over."

Catherine softened. She came close to her lover, and he held her.

"Your mother is on to us."

She kissed him. "I'll talk to her in the morning."

"Did you know about the hall cameras?"

"Doesn't everyone have them installed?"

Rowell knew somehow that he was missing something. He dropped to his knees. She hadn't responded to the love part.

"Marry me. I will try to be a good husband. Your mom told me to ask."

"Oh, god, Rowell, really you asked my mom?"

"Forget the last sentence."

She looked at him on his knees. She remembered one game, and she saw in front of her that same boy. Now he was a man.

"You will always be my star quarterback. I love you, and I'll consider a yes answer, but we must get your case dismissed."

Despite the dismal feelings in the courtroom that day, he dragged her out to the backyard swing and pushed her. She swung and the rain started.

Mrs. Wood looked out her window and saw them.

"Finally, we might get a wedding. I need to call Stella, Trixie's mother, in the morning. She might have some clever ideas."

Connie was tucked into bed by her nurse. She looked at the ceiling.

"Cyrus, our daughter is close to a yes answer. You would be proud. Thank you. We just need some help, so Rowell doesn't go to jail. You are good at communication. Put in a good word, please."

She pressed the computer screen on her wall and saw Rowell sneaking into her daughter's room. He waved at the camera. Connie smiled.

"They need to get married soon."

Mrs. Wood fell asleep. The entire household was quiet. Tomorrow could wait.

47 CATHERINE TAKES THE STAND

Rowell watched Catherine take the stand. He looked down. He wished that she wouldn't testify. He begged her to no avail. He knew the jury members were watching his every move. Today he wore a yellow tie.

After she was sworn in, she looked at him directly and smiled. His eyes misted over, but he smiled back at her. The jury could see the couple were in love. They turned to listen to what was going to transpire. The jury was very alert.

Her lawyer approached and asked her what her name was.

"My legal name is Dr. Catherine Anne Manus. However, I've also used some prior names."

"What were those prior names?"

"I was adopted by Connie and Cyrus Wood when I was five years old. My mother died in a climbing accident when I was four. Her name was Cara Manus. Her sister was Connie Wood. My mother's boyfriend was unsuccessful in trying to take care of me. Cyrus came to my rescue. They adopted me, and my name became Amber Catherine Wood."

Several members of the jury gasped.

"Amber Wood disappeared at age seventeen. Explain how you know Rowell Blackman."

"My father wanted me to experience small-town life. He felt a large city was dangerous. He was looking to retire. He bought a home in Pepin,

Wisconsin, and I started school in the eleventh grade. I met Rowell because I made the cheerleader team. He was a quarterback."

"Did you date Rowell?"

"Yes, I did. He was nice, kind, courteous, good-looking, and quite a hunk."

Rowell smiled.

"Is Rowell capable of murdering your father?"

"Never."

"You believe the shooting of your father was an accident?"

"Yes. The only thing Rowell has ever done is to protect me. He would never hurt me or my family."

The opposing side couldn't budge Catherine's testimony.

The jury went to their room to contemplate their verdict.

Catherine waited with her lawyer. The jury was back. She walked proudly into the courtroom.

The slip was passed to the judge.

"The jury finds Rowell Blackman not guilty of the murder of Cyrus Wood."

Catherine shook with relief. Her eyes watered and spilled tears. Rowell was looking at the ceiling.

The judge continued. "The jury has cited Rowell Blackman for leaving the scene. He will be sent to prison. The time is one year. He may get out earlier for good behavior."

Catherine watched as Rowell was led away. He was glad to leave the courtroom. The jail wasn't in his plan. He wished he were somewhere like in Catherine's arms.

She looked at her lawyer.

"This is the best we could hope for. We talked about this happening."

"When can I see Rowell?"

"You go home. I'll let you know."

Catherine went home and talked with her mother. Her mother squeezed her hand.

"Rowell will be fine. He is a survivor like us."

48 RELEASE

Rowell wouldn't let her visit him in prison nor let her appear at his release.

"Thanks, buddy, I appreciate your driving through rush-hour traffic. There's a barbeque place ahead."

"Shouldn't we get you home to your fiancée?"

"No, you won't take any money, and I need to buy you supper. Catherine knows I will be a little late."

The two friends ate their barbeque. He dropped Rowell off at the front door of a large home.

"Nice pad. See you, Rowell. I expect a large party when you get married."

His friend drove away.

Rowell punched the doorbell. Catherine came out, dragged him inside, and shut the door. The two lovers held each other for a long time.

"I can't believe you are here."

They moved out of the direction of the foyer camera.

"We get married as soon as possible and have a massive party later. I'm thinking of a picnic.

"Yes."

Rowell smiled. He shouted to the foyer walls.

"She said yes!"

Rowell did a little dance and banged on the walls his favorite drum song.

Mrs. Wood appeared with her nurse.

"I knew you arrived. The house is noisier when you are around. Welcome home, Rowell."

"Hello, Connie, did you hear?"

"I heard. The dead rose in the cemetery, walked around, heard the banging, and they saw the military jets overhead. I recognized the song. You are a little off on the drumbeat. The dead, however, thought there was a war, and they went back to sleep. We can make plans tomorrow."

Rowell and Catherine watched as her mother and nurse disappeared.

Catherine led her fiancée to her bedroom.

"My mother gets strange sometimes."

Rowell looked at his fiancée. "Really. I hadn't noticed."

Catherine pulled him onto the bed.

"Be serious, Rowell. You need to buy me a ring, and I need to buy you a ring."

"Seriously, after nine months, you are thinking rings! How big? No, don't answer. I'm being silly. You want huge."

Connie started giggling. She was shaking her head in agreement. Rowell took her into his arms.

"This is better. I need a shower, and then we can play. We might not surface until next week."

She watched as he went into the bathroom.

Her phone rang. She looked at her phone screen. The call was from Trixie. Catherine answered.

"I'm your best friend. What's the deal with my mom and your mom making wedding arrangements? Those two women are out of control."

"I know, Rowell was released today. I need to disappear."

"Please don't ever use that word again. Oops, I'm bothering you. Congratulations! Have fun."

"Thank you, I will."

Catherine was happy. The six-month separation had been terrible. She wasn't letting Rowell out of her sight any time soon.

She closed the drapes to her room and checked the computer to make sure the doors and windows were locked. A new security guard company was hired to keep the media and any unwanted strangers away.

Her disclosure about being the missing Amber person would generate all types of curiosity seekers. Her lawyer warned her the busses would be loaded. She talked to the air.

"We might need to leave and live in Vancouver until things calm down. Rowell will want to thank his friends before we go with a picnic."

He approached her in a warm terrycloth bathrobe.

"Let's stay and plan our marriage and picnic."

She knew there would be arguments. She could concede this one.

"I like your friends. I remember some of the names. A picnic party sounds great."

He pulled her close.

"I like you more today than yesterday. I saw the extra security. You are ahead of me."

"Yes, I know how to protect us. My father taught me well. And you taught me."

He was done talking. They turned out the lights. The night surrounded their room. Their need for each other and love took over.

Rowell was still awake when Catherine fell asleep. He looked at her. He couldn't believe she was by his side.

He thought about the past and decided the past was done. Rowell was going to live in the present. He could finally plan for their future.

ALMOST CALM

49 PICNIC LUNCH

The chef and his assistants were getting the food trays ready when Rowell stopped to talk with the chef. He handed the man twelve hats for his food crew.

"I love cooking at parties. Everyone is happy. Thank you very much for selecting my business. The hamburgers and fried fish burgers are ready. The trays of cheese, egg salad, and ham salad are ready. The fruit sticks, bags of chips, and cookies are out. The large round coolers of water and pop are set. The beer and wine trucks have arrived. We are ready."

"Good, can I try a fish sandwich?"

The chef handed him a filled bun. Rowell took a bite.

"This is delicious. How many did we order in total? Two hundred fifty each of the burgers and fish and one hundred each of the other buns."

"Do you think we have enough? I think the men will go for the egg salad and fish."

"We do have fifty extra buns and can quickly make more ham salad."

"Good. I'd rather be well-prepared."

Rowell checked the hat table and selected one that said *I love trucks*. He picked one for his wife that said *I love you*. There were twelve sayings in total on the five hundred hats. He walked to the game tent.

The large four-foot dart game would be a hit. If you missed, the board lit up and talked. There were two hundred small notepapers with small pencils to keep score. There was a music section of plastic flutes people could learn a short song and take the item home. A water tank of five different rainbow-colored rubber duckies was for the little kids. He squeaked one of the stuffed toys and picked up a bag of sugared candy.

There were tokens to use to play the game machines. At the last minute, they brought in the game machines rather than ponies.

The picnic was at their new warehouse which was still empty, and their parking lot was large enough to accommodate their party. The row of portable bathrooms stood off to the side.

He walked toward the limousine containing his new wife, Connie, and her nurse. His slacks were new as was the dress shirt.

"Hello, sweetheart. You look casual and pretty."

Catherine kissed her husband. She wore a white cotton sundress with her yellow-amber necklace and bracelet. They sealed their union in marriage three weeks earlier in a private ceremony at Connie's home. Instead of a large formal wedding and reception, they decided to have the wedding and do a fun picnic for their friends.

He watched as they chose their lunch and sat at a table of yellow balloons and red hearts. The party wouldn't start until noon. The current time was eleven o'clock. Rowell wanted his family to have time to eat and check out the game tent. When they were done eating, Connie commented.

"I've never eaten a fish sandwich so good. The fruit on a stick was the perfect dessert. Your picnic will be a hit."

"Thank you, Connie. Now we will go to the game tent before we open the party. The limousine will stay. You can go home early if you like. This party will be noisy."

Rowell noticed that Connie wore the hat stating, *I love me.* He handed his wife her hat. She smiled.

In the game tent, he showed them how to throw the darts. Connie grabbed one of the plastic flutes, a stuffed duckie, and two bags of candy.

Both laughed. They knew she hadn't yet seen the cookies. When they were done, they settled Connie and her nurse in the large lounge area of comfortable couches.

Rowell took Catherine's hand and liked the sparkle of her wedding ring on her finger.

"I'm sorry Trixie and Stella won't be here."

"Don't worry. They are having fun in Italy. We'll get together when they return."

He noted the time.

"One last chance to use the bathroom in my office. I hear the parking lot is almost full."

They disappeared and came back to the large main doors. There were parking attendants and security personnel all over the place to keep things in order and the public out.

"Are you ready?"

She held his hand. "I'm very ready!"

The guards opened the door and the first ones in line were his good friend with a date and Sheriff Edwards with his wife. After congratulations, Rowell whispered to the men.

"The egg salad and fish sandwiches are best. Follow the large arrows to the game tent. The dartboard will blow you away. You must let the kids play on occasion, so there isn't a mutiny. There was no room for the pony tent."

The men left their women, grabbed a paper plate, and began filling it with food.

The two men wore the *I love fishing* hats.

After an hour of shaking hands, Catherine and Rowell saw Connie and the nurse leave the picnic. The chattering noise in the food hall increased by four levels. They knew the game room was worse.

People sat at tables and stood under the tents outside near the drink trucks. Everyone was given two tickets each for the liquor trucks to keep things to a sane level.

After three hours, Rowell used his keys to open the two pop and water machines. The candy and nut vending machine contents disappeared in ten minutes.

He looked over at the chef. There was one tray left of ham salad sandwiches that were freshly put out. Rowell knew that was the last fifty sandwiches of food. About a dozen cookies were remaining.

He disappeared into his office and ran into his wife. She was sitting in his chair. He sat down in a guest chair.

"I'm exhausted," said Catherine.

"The food is almost gone and the drinks. There's half a case of wine. I asked the food trucks to start handing out water."

Rowell checked his watch.

"In thirty minutes, the workers will arrive to disassemble the games and tent. The chef is almost done with his work. We can leave at that time. The workers will take the other tent and potties away tomorrow."

"I liked our party."

Rowell smiled. He enjoyed every minute of the picnic.

"Thank you. I thought we could go swimming when we get home. I want to unwrap the present from Trixie and Stella."

"I thought we have agreed to no presents."

"The outside of the box shows there are water toys inside."

"Oh, no. Next year, these women want to go to Africa."

The married couple went back to the party and checked the game room. All the flutes, stuffed toys, and candy were gone. There were a few papers and pencils left near the dartboard. She walked over to the water game of floating rubber ducks.

"Weren't there seventy-five of these little duckies?"

Rowell counted.

"Yeah. Each color went to number fifteen. There were five different rainbow shades. Five duckies are left."

He turned one over.

"Nobody wanted number thirteen. He turned the rest over."

Catherine's eyes twinkled. "Let me guess. They are all thirteen."

Rowell deposited the wet ducks into her hands while she was having hysterics.

"We'll have to pay for the plastic ducks."

"The kids did have fun. We have buckets of money."

Rowell talked with security about the workers coming. He walked over to two youngsters playing the games.

"Hey, guys, ten minutes and the party will be officially over. The workers will dismantle the tent and toys. Did you have fun?"

The older boy answered.

"Best party ever! Right, Henri?"

"Well, Rob and Henri, watch your time.

Both responded, "Yes, sir."

They both wore hats saying *I love biking*. Henri kept a rubber duck in his pocket. Rowell wondered what number was selected.

Rowell turned and was surprised to see the sheriff.

"Thank you, Rowell. I took a couple of hats for my friends. I hope you don't mind."

"Bill, how about the ducks?"

"They weren't real. I left them alone. For your next picnic, buy duck decoys. I could use some new mallards."

"No, I don't mind about the hats. Aren't the decoys generic? Now go home. I want to be alone with my gorgeous and wonderful wife."

Sheriff Edwards patted him on the back.

"This picnic was a whopper. I can't wait to come to your next party. My wife is sitting in my truck. I better hurry. I think our whole town showed up. That's why the food went fast, and people stayed so long. We caught a year's worth of useful tips and gossip. Besides, everybody didn't eat breakfast before they came. You know how it is in small towns. There aren't that many good places to eat."

"I'm glad you enjoyed the show. We wanted people to feel welcome and comfortable."

The sheriff leaned over, "The best part was the dart game. I won ten rounds. Then I met and talked with your security people. Their guns are super new, and the handle grips were nice. We didn't dare shoot, too many little kids around. They let me and the wife use your office bathroom. They told me your desk was plastic, and you were going to make a lot of those desks. I want one for my garage, only thinner. Then I could sit in the shade in the summer in the garage. You let me know how much, okay?"

Rowell was pleased.

"I'll be seeing you in about two months. You've given me an idea."

The sheriff looked at his watch.

"I have to leave. Oh, my wife told me you looked different. Let me see. Yeppers, you do have a fresh look."

Rowell frowned.

"Your look is older and happy, boy. The new image works. Married and hands-off. In other words, ladies don't hit on me."

Rowell watched the two boys and his friend leave. He left the game tent to find Catherine. She was near the waiting limousine.

"All the balloons are gone from the tables?"

"I gave them to the little girls. You should have seen their faces. Sheer delight."

Rowell told her he needed a few minutes more. She nodded.

He talked to his workers and the security team. They would ensure the place was empty and secure.

The married couple rode home to swim in the house's resurfaced pool.

Connie overheard them screaming at each other. She stopped eating the fruit kebob the chef made for her. She held half a strawberry in the air. She scooted her chair to look at the noise.

"What is the object in the pool?"

The nurse looked down.

"I see a large blowup giraffe and a lion in the pool."

Connie finished the last bite of fruit.

"I have a zoo in my pool. This place is no longer stale and boring."

50 A RETURN VISIT

Rowell glanced at the bed of his truck. The items were still secured with the rope. He drove into Pepin and found one house. He backed his truck to within a foot of the garage door. He honked his horn.

The man came out.

"Rowell, how nice to see you. What in the world do you have in the back?"

"Bill, I did a prototype. I have a survey. After a month, you complete the survey and put it in the return and stamped envelope. This is a fabulous innovative design. I figured you would be truthful."

The sheriff handed the survey to his wife.

"I'm always truthful. Well, most of the time is better than not at all."

Rowell unhooked the tailgate.

"Give me a hand."

His friend guided the object in a spot near the window of his garage. Rowell unwrapped the material. He shoved the desk next to the wall.

Rowell brought out the plastic chair and took his tools. Within minutes, the chair was put together.

He unwrapped some plastic shelves and took his electric screwdriver and screws and attached the shelves to the garage walls.

Rowell stood back.

"What do you think, Bill?"

The sheriff sat at his new plastic desk and rubbed the surface.

"This is nice. What do I owe you?"

Rowell sighed. He would need to explain. "You complete the survey, and this stuff is yours to keep. No charge."

"If I don't complete the survey?"

The sheriff looked at his friend. "I'm kidding. Thanks, Rowell. Come into the house, and we can have some refreshments."

Rowell paused. He didn't want to hurt his friend's feelings.

"I have to go to another friend's house. I made smaller dartboards."

Sheriff Edwards understood.

"How much is the dartboard?"

Rowell smiled.

"We are running a survey on the modern design in six months. I'll add your name to the list of testers."

"Bless you, my friend. My dart board is so old, the darts won't stick anymore. Can I see this one?"

Rowell unwrapped the other package in his truck.

"This one is a beauty."

"We've made the inner circle a replaceable cork."

Sheriff Edwards nodded his approval.

Rowell drove to his friend's apartment across from the pier. He knocked on the door. He could hear people scrambling inside. Rowell waited until the door opened. His friend was with someone.

"Rowell, I forgot you were coming. This is Melissa, and she must leave. She owns a tiny sailboat and teaches classes."

"Hi, Melissa."

The woman left, and the two men went to the truck and brought the package into the apartment.

His friend took the old dartboard off the wall and threw it in the trash. Rowell took his battery-powered screwdriver and attached the plastic dartboard.

Rowell handed his friend the survey.

"You're the first tester. Try this one out for a month. Send the survey back."

He handed his friend the paperwork. His friend frowned.

"Ask Melissa to help you."

"Geesh, Rowell, I can read."

"I know you can read. This idea is important to me. You are always late. Even in high school, you were late for football practice. I don't want you to be late with the survey. There is a deadline date."

His friend thought about what Rowell told him.

"Thanks, man, I'll get Melissa to help me. My uniform was tight. I was late trying to squeeze my big butt into those tights. The coach finally ordered me the next size."

Rowell took out a couple of the darts. His friend did the same. They threw the darts at the board. His friend won every time.

"There's something wrong with the darts. You shouldn't have won."

His friend smiled wickedly. "I always beat you before. I can beat you with any wonder-child plastic you can build."

Rowell put the darts in the box. "Brave talk. We'll see about the next one that I build."

"Bring the game on, bro!"

Rowell left his friend's apartment and drove home. His plastic business was moving along nicely. He was profitable in the second year.

Catherine encouraged him to design more furniture and games. He had more ideas rattling around in his head.

Rowell sent a different dartboard set to his new friends, Henri, and Rob. Renee gave him their addresses three weeks before the picnic.

51 BOOK FINAL AND THE BLACKMAN'S VACATION

Renee Kendra and her husband enjoyed Catherine and Rowell Blackman's picnic. She wrote them a thank you card and enclosed the card with a copy of her recent book.

The story about Amber Wood's disappearance was finished. Renee was glad there was romance in the end. The words were easier to write than the evil parts. She hoped their life together would be calm.

Seeing the two of them at the picnic made Renee feel overwhelming relief. Although her book was fiction, what was unfolding in front of everyone at the picnic was real. Two hearts were igniting whenever they looked at each other.

Renee hugged her husband.

"The book is done?"

"Yes, and I received my wish."

He knew his wife meant the romantic part. "I guess science fiction is off the table. How about a war story?"

The dog started barking.

"See, even the dog disagrees with you," offered Renee.

After a year, Rowell and Catherine Blackman were ready for a month's vacation at a leased house in Seattle.

They sat on the leather couch and lounge chair in the room behind Rowell's warehouse office. Connie

Wood moved into a new residence with assisted living with her nurse. The furniture in the home was sold. The books went to various libraries and collectors. Most of the yellow amber specimen collection was donated to a museum.

Their clothing boxes and stuff they wanted to keep were packed and in storage. The new house they built would be complete in a month.

Connie's house was sold to her lawyer as an investment property.

"I'm glad we are staying overnight here and fly tomorrow."

Catherine watched her husband.

"Why did we need to wait a day. Our suitcases are all packed?"

Rowell checked his watch. "The food truck has arrived. I told him to come early. What would you like to eat?"

"We waited a day, so you could eat tacos?"

She laughed at his silly grin.

"You want the hamburger ones with the crunchy shell. You normally eat two. I'm having the gigantic pork burrito."

She watched as Rowell went to the truck and returned with a cardboard container of drinks and packages. His workers saw the food truck and ran outside.

"Here you go. Nice and hot."

They ate their brunch. The next day, they flew to Seattle. After three weeks of loafing around, Rowell approached his wife.

"A large toy manufacturer wants to buy my business lock, stock, and barrel in Minneapolis."

Catherine looked outside at the view. Some boaters were traveling the waterway. The trees were bright green. The area was beautiful and serene.

"The business was your idea. You can sell it if you want to. Is that why you were a little restless?"

"Yes, I told them I would sell, but I needed a year. I sign papers when we get back."

She thought about their new house.

"We probably shouldn't buy modern furniture."

"Too late, we have a hide abed couch."

He noticed her total look of surprise.

"The couch is nice and comfortable. I also bought bedding. My security people let the furniture boys in the house and deposited the bedding boxes."

"Great, we don't have to stay in a hotel."

After a week, Rowell watched as his wife packed.

"I like being a bum. This was the best fun we've enjoyed since Vancouver. I could see us doing this permanently."

They flew to Minneapolis and walked into their new house. The house plans seemed bigger. The houses were fifteen feet apart. She was used to over an acre. Catherine ordered pizza and drinks. The two people unpacked the boxes and made the couch turn into a bed.

The pizza delivery boy arrived, handed over the boxes, and left.

"Cheese, please." He selected the white sauce chicken. Bringing napkins of food, they sat on the bed and ate.

Rowell looked around. "We need drapes."

Catherine put her empty napkin down and took a large sticky notepad from her purse. She placed the sticky notes over the bottom portion of the window.

"We're covered."

What she didn't see was the nosy new neighbor staring at her sticky notes. The neighbor rudely called the homeowner's association and reported the violation.

52 DRAPES AND A MOVE

The drapery van pulled away from the curb as Rowell drove his truck into the driveway. He pulled into his empty garage and went into the house.

"How's my girl?"

"Fine. They said new drapes take three months. I ordered a shade for the den. They found one in stock and hung the shade today."

Rowell looked in the den. The sticky notes were gone. In their place was a green shade.

"You hate green."

"I know. The shade was a return and was cheap. It's white on the other side."

"At least our neighbor will be happy."

"I doubt she will. She thrives on stress. I don't think she likes children."

Rowell's phone rang. He sat down on a folding chair and made some notes.

She overheard his conversation.

"No, there isn't anyone who comes to mind. This is terrible news. I'll talk with Catherine. We'll be careful."

She sat down on the other folding chair. He explained to her the strange news.

"I can't believe some person burned down my mother's old house. I'm glad we weren't there and were in our home."

"The lawyer didn't seem too extremely upset. He said the only thing he lost was some new paint. This way, he can turn the land into two lots. His insurance will cover the loss. He wanted to make sure we were safe."

"The arsonist must not have known that we moved."

Rowell moved his chair closer and took Catherine's hands. "Do you know of anyone who might torch a house?"

Catherine remembered when she first moved to Pepin.

"There was some hushed talk about a girl who was temporarily home. You were at football camp."

Rowell scratched his head. He didn't know of any names.

"I saw someone near the school with matches. I went inside and told the principal. Then I went home."

"Belinda talked about a person crazier than her."

"I don't remember the girl's name who had the matches. No one told me," said Catherine.

Rowell thought and he suddenly remembered. He dialed Connie's lawyer and gave him the name.

"Should we leave the area?"

"No, I think they will find her. Her name is Bella Dawson, Bev's sister. She liked to light fires too much. She wore tank tops that sometimes read, *Get Lit, Fire Starter, Burn Baby, etc.*"

He finished his call.

"As a teenager, she disappeared a lot with her mother's car which made the mom pretty mad. One year, she enrolled in an expensive exercise class in

Minnesota with her mother's credit card which added more fuel. Pardon my pun! The mother finally sent Bella away. I believe she went to five places total. The therapy sessions paid for by the county didn't work."

The police found Bella with her boyfriend. They took pictures of the houses they torched. The address was written in magic marker. The pictures were on the walls in their apartment as trophies.

The police also found devices for starting fires in the closets. The couple wasn't getting out of jail anytime soon, nor would they get sent to a cushy insane asylum. Anyone who could build the fire starters was smart, and they would be treated like the other half-normal idiots that committed crimes.

Catherine and Rowell knew the couple saw their names in the paper during his trial. The fire starters targeted Connie's house. They were relieved Bella Dawson, and her boyfriend was locked away.

The next day Rowell brought home some large sandwiches and a basket of fruit.

"We need to talk. We have five months left before the warehouse and my business closes. I don't need to be here to handle things. My foremen do a good job."

"I want to move, too."

"Good. I've contacted a realtor. She has a young couple with four children who might be interested. Her husband is a wrestler and makes good money. Their dog's name is Bernard. They've driven the neighborhood six times. Their parents live close by.

Our house seems to be an ideal fit due to the gated large backyard."

Catherine snickered.

"Bernard is an interesting name. Do the kids own bikes?"

"Yes, and the husband likes to tinker with boat engines in his spare time. She told me they have lots of friends with boats."

"The next-door neighbor will go nuts."

"I'm not going to care. We'll be in Seattle or Vancouver. Your choice."

"Vancouver."

In a month, they were gone. They left the hide abed and green shade. Catherine called the drapery place and paid extra for the rush order. The drapes were installed the day before they left.

On the way out of the housing area, they saw the large moving van and a huge SUV. The SUV was bright apple green and filled with noisy kids.

"Their vehicle matches the shade," said Catherine.

One of the kids was hanging out the window with a remote-control airplane. The little girl showed her talking plastic horse to another little girl in the neighborhood on a tricycle. Two other kids were running a contest of how many tissues they could get out the window before anybody noticed.

The piece de resistance was the large Bernard dog drooling out the back window. He was a St. Bernard and well-behaved around children. Catherine read those dogs only barked on occasion.

Rowell looked in the rearview mirror and saw the litter on the road and the mowed green lawns. The big dog was peeing on a newly planted pine tree.

"I'll miss this neighborhood. I liked the kids, especially the big guy. His mom was cool. She used a megaphone to call her children to lunch until someone we won't name complained."

"Oh, look, there are a bunch more kids with a lemonade stand. That is so sweet. They are charging fifty cents a glass."

"No, Catherine, we don't need any lemonade."

He handed her a can of opened iced tea.

"I'll share it. The green SUV has stopped, and the kids are climbing out."

Catherine looked back at the neighborhood scene. The kids from the lemonade stand were running to watch the mover truck, and the hyperactive new neighbors piled out of their vehicle.

She saw their next-door neighbor lady outside. She was pointing at the dog who was now in a squat position.

As they passed the guard gate, they looked over and saw three trucks pulling boats.

Rowell said, "I believe the buyers' friends have arrived. The realtor texted me. Our buyers received approval for a small move-in party."

They both felt relieved. "We left in the nick of time," commented Rowell.

"I don't know, the party might have been entertaining. There are food and ants at a party. Our former neighbor lady hates ants. She was always outside spraying."

She watched as an ice cream truck turned into their neighborhood. Catherine saw the look on her husband's guilty face.

"They have chocolate ice cream sandwiches. There was a disclaimer. The ants love their chocolate milk products."

Catherine said, "You're bad."

"Sugar is good."

The truck pulled into the buyer's driveway and drove onto the grass. "You're still bad."

Rowell smiled.

"Always."

53 VANCOUVER

"I think that I'd like to buy a new sports car. We don't need a truck anymore. There's a little leakage of oil. Not too much, but enough to be a problem. I could fix the leak."

They were driving in his truck to Vancouver. Catherine knew his methodology and approach were a little sneaky.

"You buy the nicest sports car you can find."

"I will. Thank you."

"We should find a summer place further south. The winter here is snowy."

Rowell thought about the cold.

"You look, and I'll help decide."

The Blackman family's life in Vancouver settled down as soon as they bought contemporary furniture. Catherine and Rowell decided life was meant to be positive. Their energy was focused on relaxation and fun. He missed the food truck and his workers, but he loved Catherine more.

He came home to their high-rise apartment with a bouquet of yellow sunflowers.

"Your choice of cream-colored drapes is much more our style. They go with the curved leather couch. The red coral-colored pillows add a nice touch. The yellow fish pillow is my favorite. I'm a little afraid to sit in the yellow chair. The cognac-colored chair is bigger. Does the designer do whales?"

Catherine was adding more water to the vase and rearranging the stems.

"These are pretty flowers. I bet they came from the fields we saw near Nelson."

"How did you know?"

She showed him the tag attached inside.

"Do you miss being there?" asked Rowell.

"No."

"I love you." He kissed his wife.

She kissed him back. "I love you more because I found this cool restaurant today."

He waited and watched her take a package out of a bag.

"No, you didn't? Gimmie, gimmie." He could hardly contain his excitement.

"You are easy to satisfy. Big heart and an even bigger stomach. The designer doesn't do whales because everybody who is not important does the whale thing. Yes, my tacos are still in the bag."

She watched his eyes as he bit into the gigantic burrito. The cheese and beans oozed out. He licked around the outside as the rice and pork fell out.

"Perfect!"

She crunched on her tacos.

"You usually eat the crunchy tacos, but this burrito is fantastic."

Catherine knew her life was as close as she could come to perfection. Rowell was her everything. She never wanted to disappear. There was no reason.

He looked at the bag and napkins.

"There's no name."

Catherine confessed, "I switched the bags and tossed the napkins because they were soaked with juice. Besides, only I know where the restaurant is located."

"Oh, no, you don't." He grabbed her tacos and held them in the air.

She screamed and tried to reach them. He was taller than her. She punched his stomach lightly. He grunted with pleasure. Catherine confessed.

"I used the magnet on the refrigerator and put their menu underneath. Let go of my tacos and see for yourself."

He dropped her tacos on the table. She dived for the filled wrappers. Rowell watched her eat, and the juice ran down her chin. He walked to the refrigerator and grabbed the menu off the side. He read and groaned louder.

"They have fried burritos with green sauce. The menu says their green sauce is made fresh daily. The green sauce is the best usually. I can't remember the last time I ate fried burritos. We are most definitely going to eat there. How about this evening?"

"No, tomorrow is soon enough."

She walked to the refrigerator and pulled out the can.

Rowell frowned, "Whipped Cream?"

"We have peaches, too. The store finally has the white ones you like. I thought in the morning you could make us some waffles.

Rowell relaxed and took another bite. He was enjoying the conversation and his burrito.

"Waffles always work. The white peaches are almost as good as the marionberries."

He winked at her. She hugged her husband and put the can in the refrigerator.

Rowell was taking a yellow highlighter and marking the menu.

"These are the selections we will want to eat. We can give the order to the waitress the second we sit down."

"Type A personality?"

Rowell looked at his wife. "Too much?"

"Overboard."

He put the yellow marker down and slapped the menu under the magnet. He returned to her.

She sat in his lap. He held his beautiful wife. The menu and food were forgotten.

Their life was going to be easy. Their future seemed attainable. There was no need to paint a wish on a wall.

Rowell set his wife down. "I forgot your present."

He disappeared into their bedroom and handed her a new pair of binoculars. Rowell pulled her outside their patio doors. He was like an excited child.

The sun formed a yellow amber sphere as the color drifted toward the ocean water.

"Hurry look at the sun. The lens is specially designed to avoid dangerous reflections. The sun looks like your amber ball."

She watched and handed him the binoculars. When the molten yellow sun disappeared, he turned. They kissed.

"That was wonderful."

She could see Rowell's happy face.

"I bought my pair. The price was terrible, but I knew you wouldn't mind. We can watch it again tomorrow."

Catherine loved the last word. There would be many tomorrows to share.

"I can hardly wait."

"Oh, one more present. The writer talked with Gisele Rivers about your favorite yellow ball. She looked in the boxes from her husband's office. Guess what!"

Catherine wasn't sure but was hopeful.

"And?"

He handed her the yellow ball with the line that looked like a river. She gasped. The warmth from the smooth ball made her feel giddy with relief. His eyes were filled with joy that she liked the present.

"Thank you." The yellow ball was placed inside a glass case where it belonged.

She was barely listening to her husband's chatter about a potential upcoming whale watching trip.

Catherine was enjoying the moment. Realization struck her. He moved to Vancouver for her. She could tell he missed his business and friends. The apartment could be their escape on occasion. She stopped him with a touch of her hand.

"We should go back."

Rowell stopped. "What?"

"I think we should have another picnic while we live there. You could design some new games for our friends."

He looked at his wife. "You are sure?"

She beamed brightly.

"Perfect!"

Her husband raced to the den. She could hear him talking to himself about a pinwheel with mallards.

She could see ping pong balls flying off the wheel of the prototype. They would need to rent a warehouse and equipment.

Her husband came back to the kitchen for a cola. He gave her another smooch.

"The first design will blow them away."

Catherine watched as he left. Rowell was busy. She would give him a couple of hours to play with his designs. She stepped outside for a minute to stare at the heavens. The stars filled the skies. Catherine went inside.

Rowell looked up from his computer in the den.

"Don't forget little girls like yellow flowers, red hearts, and shooting stars with blue tails."

Rowell wrote the words on his notepad.

"Don't be too long."

Catherine knew the way to her man's heart. Silence would never be in the room when the two of them were together.

Author's List of Books

Yellow Amber and Missing Person

Blue Dancer and the Dark

Purple Queen and Lost Charm

Knight Detective Series:
Book 1 - Gray Area for a Woman
Book 2 – Pink Sky in the Morning

Orange Carousel and Orchid Murders

Black Horse and Female Lawyer

Green Emeralds and Heist Club

White Boom and the Seagulls

Gold and the Spotted Jaguar

Raiment Red and a Raven –
A Southwest Mystery

A Wright Series:
Book 1 – Diamonds Blondes and Poison
Book 2 – Dead On Coordinates
Book 3 – Wild Golden Obsession
Book 4 – No Easy Target
Book 5 – Powerhouse Race
Book 6 – Cross Paths